"Hang on, Jeremy!"

Ruby clenched her jaw, tamped down her fear and clambered up the stairs using her hands and feet. They wobbled precariously. Her breath caught in her throat.

She could see Jeremy as he tried to lever himself out of the hole. But his effort splintered the wood on the edges, causing the hole to widen.

A slow creak sent chills down her spine. The fire-weakened flooring around him sagged. It was a matter of time before it gave way completely.

Her stomach roiled and the incapacitating images that visited whenever she confronted heights exerted an unnerving power. Then Ruby's eyes widened. The suspect had turned back, as if to help Jeremy regain his footing. *He's going to save him.*

Ruby lurched toward the men. But she couldn't trust the floor to hold her weight. The suspect jerked his head up and backed away from Jeremy.

It's all up to me.

But if she attempted to cross the floor to grab Jeremy's arm and hoist him up, they would both plummet to certain death.

Carol Newhouse is a member of many writing organizations, including Sisters in Crime, the Writer's Support Group and Book Club (Texas), and the Faith, Hope and Love Christian Writers group. When not hard at work writing, reading or participating in virtual exercise classes, she enjoys painting with watercolors, playing competitive bridge, walking her dog and hanging out at the Toronto Zoo. This is her debut novel for Love Inspired Suspense.

Books by Carol Newhouse

Love Inspired Suspense

Hidden Colorado Danger

Visit the Author Profile page at LoveInspired.com.

HIDDEN COLORADO DANGER

CAROL NEWHOUSE

LOVE INSPIRED SUSPENSE
INSPIRATIONAL ROMANCE

LOVE INSPIRED® SUSPENSE
INSPIRATIONAL ROMANCE

ISBN-13: 978-1-335-63867-0

Hidden Colorado Danger

Copyright © 2025 by Carol Newhouse

Love Inspired
22 Adelaide St. West, 41st Floor
Toronto, Ontario M5H 4E3, Canada
www.LoveInspired.com

Printed in Lithuania

MIX
Paper | Supporting
responsible forestry
FSC® C021394

For I know the thoughts that I think toward you,
saith the Lord, thoughts of peace, and not of evil,
to give you an expected end.
—*Jeremiah* 29:11

For my sister who has been with me
every step of the writing journey.

ONE

It was a night so dark Sheriff Ruby Prescott could barely see her hand in front of her face. Concealed behind the low branches of a squat pinyon pine, she stared at the Grand Theater for any signs of life. Nothing. She licked her lips and shifted her weight from one foot to the other.

An owl screeched. A breeze swept through the pines. Ruby shivered. Standing in Colorado's October weather near midnight held little appeal, but information about a suspected break-in had forced her out of her warm office on this moonless night.

She wondered why the caller who reported a possible prowler hadn't identified themselves but hoped this might be the opportunity to catch the person whose serial burglaries had dogged Tinker for the past three months.

There. A pinpoint of light in a ground-floor window moved slowly, stopped and moved again. Something or someone was inside. Still she waited. She had to be sure. Move too quickly, the intruder would slip out the exit or double-back behind her leaving an empty building to investigate. Too late and the newspaper headlines would scream "Sheriff Watches While Historic Theater Burgled."

A loose window frame caught by a gust of wind banged against the side of the long-ago retired building. The noise provided cover. She said her silent prayer asking God to look after everyone's safety, then scooted across the grass past the barricaded door. She squeezed behind the frame and hoisted herself onto the windowsill. Once her feet touched the floorboards, she unclipped her tactical flashlight and flicked it to high beam. The flood of light illuminated what had been the theater's front of house.

Straight ahead, she knew the double doors would open to reveal the auditorium, row upon row of upholstered seats divided into three sections by two aisles spanning its length. But anything of value to a thief would be found in the rooms behind the stage at the back.

Ruby snapped off her flashlight, cracked open the auditorium door and slipped inside. The ghost light, a single bulb traditionally left on to comfort theater ghosts and as a safety measure to prevent falls into the orchestra pit, cast a dim glow over the stage.

She spied a stepladder positioned underneath a hanging cord. It looked as if someone had been interrupted while changing a stage light, but the theater had closed its doors decades earlier, and she recalled the building owner only paid Teddy Hume the minimum to perform rudimentary maintenance checks.

Ruby gazed up at the network of lighting grids and considered the possibility of climbing the stairs toward the sound booth, crossing a catwalk to the front of the auditorium, then dropping down on the intruder. She could use the element of surprise to her advantage, but her dislike of heights made her nix the idea.

Instead, she crouched and began to creep up the aisle. Ten rows from the front, she froze. Someone stepped onto the stage and approached the furled curtain. Ruby ducked behind the chairs to watch and wait. The person examined the rolled cloth, but after only a few minutes grunted. They pulled the stepladder to the curtain.

The burly figure dressed all in black wore a ski mask to completely cover his face and hair. Medium height ruled out the maintenance man, who stood well over six feet.

Ruby stifled an urge to sneeze and dug her fingers into her thighs. Her muscles began to tighten, the first sign of cramps, and she longed to stand and stretch. She imagined jumping up, drawing her weapon and ordering the person to stop, but her preference to keep her gun holstered unless the situation included a threat to human life quashed the thought. Instead, she stood and yelled, "Sheriff Prescott speaking. You are trespassing. Give yourself up, now."

His response was to turn and run.

Ruby regretted not having a deputy as backup, but with pursuit her only alternative, she tore down the aisle and up onto the stage.

The two rooms alongside the stage contained a lot of clutter but there was no sign of anyone. She slammed on the brakes at the end of the hall. A small window silhouetted the prowler, who had a foot on the sill to use as an anchor and was in the process of hauling his body through it. The other leg dangled down the wall.

Ruby lunged, grabbed the ankle and pulled backward. The intruder wrenched his foot sideways, then slammed it against the wall in an attempt to dislodge her hands. Pain shot through her fingers and up her arms, but she didn't loosen her grip. Ruby dug her heels into the floor and threw her weight back again. But this time, instead of resisting, the intruder changed direction and catapulted backward. The air whooshed out of her. Both tumbled onto the floor in a tangle of arms and legs.

The rollover trapped Ruby underneath. She wriggled but remained pinned. When she felt hands close around her throat, she panicked, but attempts to shift the weight on her chest or break the chokehold failed. She willed herself to stop the struggle and forced her body to sag, feigning a loss of consciousness.

She heard a grunt, and the weight crushing her lessened. The intruder stood. Ruby counted to ten, then rolled sideways and heaved herself to her feet. They faced each other. Then the intruder hunched his shoulders, ducked his head and ran straight toward her. He aimed his head at her chest, but Ruby, who had been trained to defend herself against such an attack, grabbed his shoulders and used his momentum to heave him into the air.

They crashed into the floor again, but by the time she righted herself and spun around, he leapt from a squat in an attempt to grab her gun from its holster. She kicked the underside of his chin. When she heard a yelp and realized she'd connected, she clamped her hands onto her holster, turned her left hip away, and twisted to thrust her right hip forward. The movements saved her gun, but she lost her balance.

The intruder pushed past Ruby. Though her legs quivered, she struggled up. She saw a vacant hallway, but realized with a start that the intruder had not taken the opportunity to flee the theater. She could hear scraping in one of the side rooms.

Again she wished for backup but drew her gun from its holster. Things had escalated quickly from investigating a possible prowler. Ruby stood in the doorway of the second prop room and shouted, "I repeat, I'm Sheriff Prescott. Give it up now."

The intruder slowed, then stopped rooting through the rack of costumes, turned to face her and held up gloved hands in surrender. But as she unclipped her handcuffs and stepped into the room, he bent behind a trunk on the floor and gave a mighty push. She tried to dodge the sliding box, but as it rammed her ankle, the lid popped open and she tripped. As she toppled into it, two bony arms shot up. She recoiled horrified. Bad enough to fight with a prowler, but to wrestle with a skeleton? Not today.

Ruby shoved the bones off to the side, but by the time she scrambled to her feet, the intruder had raced out of the room to freedom.

Crime analyst Jeremy Lawson was unhappy. Five years of climbing the corporate ladder turned to dust, all because one of his composites led the police to the wrong suspect. Who knew he'd be forced to trade New York City for Tinker, Colorado?

He took in four bare walls, a battered desk with a lone chair and five filing cabinets. A large whiteboard with scribbles and a layer of dust was propped in one corner. Stacks of files, Standard Operating Procedure binders and official-looking manuals completed the decor.

County Commissioner Tom Ewan's words still

rang in his ears. "This should suit your needs.
Our sheriff's office may not be your usual digs,
but you'll love it in no time. Any problems, report
them directly to me, okay? Ruby Prescott's a fine
law enforcement officer, but she can be a bit full
of herself. Just remember, she may be your immediate boss, but I promised your supervisor I'd
take care of you."

Interesting welcome speech. Jeremy sat on the
wooden chair. When he swiveled, it emitted a low-
grade squeak. When he rolled it over to the filing
cabinets, the wheels squealed. He began opening
the cabinet drawers to examine their contents and
soon buried his head in a report. Someone cleared
their throat.

Jeremy jumped and cranked his head toward
the door.

"Settling in, are we?"

A woman blocked the frame. She stood tall in
her cowboy boots. Sandy curls were tied into a
ponytail and she had perched a Western hat atop
her head. Broad cheekbones. Straight eyebrows.
Lips thinned into a frown. Attractive despite a
no-nonsense demeanor.

He shoved the report back in the cabinet, rose
and extended his hand, eager to dispel any negative appearance his position, hunched over an
open drawer burrowing into the cabinet, may have
conveyed.

"Jeremy Lawson."

"All the way from New York City."

"Affirmative."

"And already, you've commandeered our re-cords room and made yourself comfortable by snooping into files."

"Not exactly. I've met a commissioner who wel-comed me and gave me this, um, office." Even to his ears, the rationale sounded like a weak excuse.

"Tom Ewan, no doubt." Her frown deepened. "I would've been here, but I had to touch base with my investigators who are out processing a crime scene. Well, I'm not sure where I'll put you, but it won't be here. Let's go to my office."

Jeremy followed her to a larger room across the hall.

"First things first—" Ruby pointed to the com-puter on her desk "—we've got one of these for each station, including the records room and a sixth one stashed in a box, all refurbished. The budget doesn't allow me to buy a new computer for you, although if you're on cozy terms with Commissioner Tom Ewan, you may get authori-zation for extra dollars."

Jeremy heard an undertone of contempt in her voice.

She picked up a pen. "How many technological gadgets do you need?"

Jeremy remembered the smartphones, tablets and computers with access to dozens of software tools at his fingertips back in New York. "I can work with one of your computers."

"Good."

When Ruby spoke, her voice rose and she looked past him instead of at him. He recognized the classic signs of resentment and wondered whether they signaled anger at technology in general or at his presence.

"Now, where will I put you?"

"I can share space. I'm happy in a corner of the main office. Always better to be in the loop, not sequestered."

Ruby gazed at her desktop and tapped her pencil against her coffee mug as she considered her options. "You want a window?"

"No. I prefer an inside wall. Better to face the outer door and the hallway and keep my back to the wall so I can see what's coming."

"Cop's answer. You make it easy."

"I try."

"Okay. Let's get you set up."

Ruby moved to the front office and, with the help of Deputy Bill Kirk, charged with manning the station, dragged a desk out of a corner and positioned it as per Jeremy's instructions. Refurbished computers and second-hand desks reminded Jeremy of how far away he was from New York.

She took a computer from a box in the corner. "Was your job in New York primarily internal?"

"I patrolled the Bronx my first two years. When they needed someone to train as an analyst, I stepped up, but I didn't expect it to become a niche. I've wanted to get out from behind the desk more often for some time now. One of the reasons I agreed to this transfer."

Agreed? Hah. I really wasn't given much choice.

"Well, our force is responsible for policing Tinker and the larger county.

"I don't intend to put you on patrol, but I can use an extra pair of eyes and hands when I work the more complex cases, a luxury I can't afford with only three deputies. I'll keep them on their usual schedule. You can divide your time between shadowing me and conducting your crime analysis."

Jeremy flexed his biceps and grinned. "Glad to be out in the field again, even if it is only temporary. Good thing I kept up my membership at the gym."

Ruby didn't smile. "We share cars from a small fleet of SUVs built for the terrain. Now here's a list of important names and numbers to program into your smartphone. After that, get familiar with everything while I write up a report."

Dismissed, Jeremy followed Ruby's instructions, then looked around the front office. Not much happening. Time to get some air. His stomach rumbled, and it occurred to him that he hadn't had anything to eat since he'd arrived that morning. He hoped the town had a decent diner.

He nodded to the deputy and walked out the front door over to his sports car parked in the lot. He patted the red hood and kept his voice low. "Sorry, girl, it's the parking lot for you while I'm working. Seems your build doesn't suit my new boss."

He straightened. *Lord, why am I here?* The plateaus of the Flat Top Mountains in the distance to his right didn't offer any answers, but they created a different sight line than the concrete and glass monuments he'd grown accustomed to in New York City.

The commercial area, which featured a number of businesses, stretched to his left, and he considered walking the short distance for a snack, then dismissed the idea. He turned back to the office in time to see the sheriff throw open the door and stride out.

"Urgent call from Deputy Martinez. Someone's breached my crime scene. Let's go."

TWO

Jeremy took a deep breath to counter his surge in adrenaline. He wondered if sitting in the passenger seat beside Sheriff Ruby Prescott could explain his rise in body heat and glanced sideways.

Ruby sat ramrod straight, hands on the steering wheel, eyes fixed on the road.

Jeremy cleared his throat. "Does this happen often, someone tampering with a crime scene?"

"Never. I always secure the scene with tape and post a deputy. There's never been a breach, so I've got to ask myself what makes this time different?"

"The discovery of a skeleton?"

"No one knows about our bones, yet. The burglary was a statistic in the morning crime report, so if anything, the only assumption out there is that I foiled an intrusion by a person unknown."

"You never know how people react."

"I do. I've lived in Tinker most of my life. I pride myself in understanding the people here, how they think and how they'll act."

Jeremy fell silent.

At the outskirts of town, Ruby turned up a lane dotted with overgrown weeds pushing through snow-covered cracks in the uneven pavement and stopped the car in front of what looked to be a converted barn. Jeremy could imagine the theater in its glory days. The sign over the double doors hung slightly askew, but even the faded paint on the wooden frame couldn't detract from the effect of two masks, one happy and one sad, fashioned out of copper with brass trim fastened over the two-and-a-half-story entrance.

"Takes your breath away. It's been how many years?"

Ruby paused to think. "At least fifty. This place shut down long before I was born."

Deputy Martinez stood to the left of the building, an older woman beside him.

"Lucille Trefor, no surprise I guess." Ruby groaned and stepped out of the car.

The woman identified as Lucille topped out at the deputy's shoulder. She brushed a few strands of windblown white hair off her forehead and crinkled her blue eyes as she looked over to the squad car and smiled.

"Good morning, Sheriff. He asked me to come back outside, so here I am."

"You admit being inside?" Ruby raised both eyebrows.

"Oh, yes indeed."

"Didn't you notice the yellow tape? It clearly says, 'Do Not Cross.'"

"Of course I saw it, but why would it apply to me?"

"Why wouldn't it?"

"I own the place." Lucille held a key aloft.

"You think ownership gives you the right to ignore the Do Not Cross tape?"

Lucille thrust her jaw forward. "I wanted to see what last night's excitement was all about. I needed to inspect the theater for damage."

"You didn't think by tramping through the property you might be destroying evidence?"

Lucille hung her head. "No. Sorry." Her lower lip began to quiver.

"Lucille, please don't cry. Just tell me where you went."

"Through the front door." Lucille pointed.

Ruby tipped her head. "It's barricaded. They all are."

"Oh my, that's only for show. The timber bisecting that particular door covers the keyhole, but it lifts right up. Don't let on. I'd hate to have a parade of people on the property."

Ruby grimaced. "Information I could have used last night. So once you went in…?"

"I started up the side stairs leading to the sound booth, but with an inch of dust on each step, I could tell no one had climbed them in ages. Then I turned around and went through the auditorium door. I only got halfway down the aisle when Deputy Martinez corralled me and asked me to come with him." She heaved a sigh of resignation.

"I was around the back of the theater when she arrived, or I'd have seen her and stopped her sooner," the deputy interrupted. "Sorry, boss."

Ruby folded her arms across her chest and took one step closer to Lucille. "You didn't touch anything?"

"No, well maybe I placed a hand on a seat back to steady myself. The aisle's a bit steep and the carpet's a bit torn. And your deputy gave me a start, but otherwise, as they say, I kept my hands in my pockets."

Ruby pushed her hat back. "Lucille, we'll need to ask you a few questions. This is Officer Jeremy Lawson, by the way. He's not a deputy, but he'll be helping me with some of my cases."

"Pleased to meet you, Jeremy." Lucille extended her hand.

Jeremy cupped hers in his, adjusting his grip to accommodate the frail fingers. "My pleasure, ma'am."

"Lucille, why don't you go back across the street to your house and wait for us while we look around inside. We'll be along shortly."

"Okay. I'll brew tea. You can take the key. Just make sure I get it back." Lucille winked before turning and trundling up the gravel driveway toward the road and her home.

Jeremy turned to look at Ruby. "She seems innocuous."

"Ha. She's one of the worst gossips in Tinker. Her nickname's 'Queen of the Rumor.'"

"Could make her a good witness."

"You think?" Ruby strode to the window at the side of the theater. "We'll use the key, but first I want to show you how I gained entry last night. You can see the screen is loose, which made it easy enough for me to squeeze inside." She grasped the screen and pulled it out to demonstrate. "I figured the prowler entered and exited the same way, although if he knew about the bogus barricade and had a key, he might have used the door."

"I doubt he went in the front door. Look." Jeremy pointed. Three nails had been ground into the dirt, nails that matched three holes on the wooden window frame.

"So he created his own entrance." Ruby took several photos of the area then withdrew a paper bag from her pocket and carefully collected the nails. "And I took the loose screen last night as a failure of the maintenance man to keep up with repairs. Let's survey the ground around the theater once more, just to make sure there's nothing else."

But there was nothing else to find.

They moved to the entrance. Jeremy easily lifted the barrier and Ruby inserted the key. The barricade slid back to its original position as the door swung open.

Ruby entered the foyer, then peered outside. "From this angle, I can see how everything would appear intact once the door is closed again."

Jeremy confirmed Ruby's observation. "The wood is so light it must be hollow, and it doesn't extend beyond the door's width. Like Lucille said, just for show."

Jeremy bent over and examined the door hinges. "No squeak here, oiled with no rust."

When Jeremy shut the door, the foyer was plunged into darkness. As he reached into his pocket for his pencil light, Ruby unclipped the large flashlight from her belt and hit the switch.

They followed the route Ruby had traveled down the auditorium aisle. Jeremy struggled to keep his focus on the worn carpet instead of letting it stray to the overhead catwalks shrouded in shadows. He wondered why she chose to sneak up on the prowler using the path most visible from the stage instead of working her way across the ceiling.

A loud crack startled him. *Don't overreact. Take one old theater and add mice.*

"Coming?" Ruby glanced back at him.

"Sure." He quickened his pace to catch up, but as he stepped forward, his heel hit a patch of bare floor. He teetered, lost his balance and fell.

"Jeremy!"

He heard an undertone of anguish in her voice. "Is anything broken?"

"I don't think so." He sucked in air, then bent each leg and rotated his ankles slowly, thankfully.

"Let me help." Ruby extended both hands.

As Jeremy hoisted himself up, his left heel began to slip again. "What's going on?" He leaned down and touched the floor underneath his foot, then rubbed his fingers together. "Someone put soap on the floor. How'd that get there?"

"Hmm." Ruby frowned. "A small amount. If it was there last night, I missed stepping in it." She examined the spot more closely. "Two possibilities come to mind. Either we've got an enthusiastic maintenance man, or someone is trying to throw us off our game by interfering with our investigation."

Jeremy thought a moment. "Probably the maintenance man. How likely is sabotage? I'm sure it was an accident. Let's keep going."

Once onstage, he turned. "The burglar bent over here?" When Jeremy touched the red, velour curtain and sash, a dust cloud wafted up his nose. He stifled a sneeze.

"Historically, costume jewelry pinned the ends of the sash together to bind the curtains after a show's run," Ruby said. "Could attract a thief."

"Do you really think a prowler would break in to check out costume jewelry? Big risk for a small reward."

"True. Maybe the person thought they'd find a king's ransom."

Jeremy scratched his head. "Stories of hidden treasure? Precious gems camouflaged among the paste? I guess anything is possible."

"You don't sound convinced. Anyway, after I startled him, he beelined down this hall, past two side rooms, to get away from me." Ruby moved to the back of the theater and into a small square room, empty save for a window. Streaks of fingerprint powder dotted its sill and frame.

"Do you think the prowler possessed rudimentary knowledge of this layout?"

"Yes, I do. The window drew him like metal to a magnet."

"You refer to the prowler as him."

"Right. At first I thought the prowler could be a medium-built man or a burly woman. But after we fought, I remembered the feel of the hands around my throat. Large hands, thick fingers. They belonged to a male. I'm sure of it."

Ruby tapped the side of her cheek before continuing, "He also wore a pair of transparent surgical gloves and had no rings, tattoos or other distinguishing marks on his hands or wrists. But despite two prolonged encounters, that's all I can tell you."

"Maybe we'll get lucky and find the mask or the gloves thrown away in the bushes."

Ruby pursed her lips. "I doubt it. The team went

over the grounds and now we've repeated the process. It's true we've got the nails pulled from the screen outside, which I missed on my first go-round, but so far this guy hasn't made many mistakes."

Jeremy closed his eyes a moment. Ruby's idiosyncratic habit of tapping her cheek while she thought drew attention to her high cheekbones and distracted him. He squeezed his eyes shut a second time, tamped down the image and wondered why each interaction with this taciturn woman made his head spin.

A smudge on the wallpaper caught Jeremy's eye, so he squatted, bent forward and reached for his pocket knife.

"If you want a sample for evidence, please ask a member of our team." Ruby's voice cut like a sword between his shoulder blades. He straightened and balanced on the balls of his feet.

"Of course," he muttered and repocketed his knife. "Where to next?"

"We fought in front of the door. He choked me almost to unconsciousness, then bolted down the hall as I struggled to my feet."

Jeremy stared at the wooden floor. No sign of the struggle remained. Still, he had to make sure all possible sources of evidence were collected, which included traces of fibers or dust invisible to the naked eye. "Let's confirm the team vacuumed all sections of the route."

"Yes, of course." Ruby's voice pitched higher.

Jeremy swallowed and followed her to the prop room door. *This is not going well.*

Two remaining members of the investigation team were inside taking photographs of the shelves filled with boxes and costumes hanging on racks.

Ruby spoke quietly. "Pictures of the trunk's exterior and interior were snapped before it was shipped to the state's forensic anthropologist. Its contents included the bones partially clothed in a polyester-type fabric, a scarf and one pink earring. You can see the photos back at the station." He could tell the trunk's dimensions from the tape outline on the floor in front of them. Ruby spoke to one of the men, who nodded when she pointed to the area they'd left.

The smell of cinnamon filled the space and tickled Jeremy's throat. He realized the teasing scent must be Ruby's shampoo. And for a moment, memories of fall overtook his thoughts. Apple pie and sticky buns, mulled wine and blue cheese. But just as quickly, the dust piled between the boxes save for one smeared rectangle, proof of the place the trunk had called home for almost fifty years, reminded him why he was here.

Once the two investigators finished processing the crime scene, Jeremy paced the room. He took three running strides forward and reached to his left. Wait. Something was wrong. Ruby had said when she appeared at the door, the prowler was sorting through the costumes at the other end of the room. He'd started from the wrong direction.

Now, Jeremy stepped alongside the costumes, then turned to face the doorway, took two running strides forward and reached to his right. "Economy of movement dictated he reach down to where the trunk had sat and pull and swing his arms to move the obstruction into the path of anyone coming into the room."

"Your point is?"

"Something I developed when I worked as a detective to get into the perp's head. At a crime scene I position myself so I can see exactly what they saw right before they left the area. If it's a murder, I'll stand beside the body and do a slow three-sixty to scan the area."

"Does it help?"

"Sometimes. I'd wondered if our prowler chose the trunk with a skeleton for a reason. Maybe he knew there'd be something inside to distract you. But I think physics explains why he grabbed it. Closest mobile object, nothing more."

"We don't have much to go on, and there's no apparent link between the skeleton and the burglaries." Ruby grimaced. "We'll know more once we assess the evidence collected here and get the report from the forensic anthropologist."

She stared, mesmerized by the space where the

trunk last rested. Jeremy saw her lips move but could barely hear her whisper.

"At first, I figured the skeleton was plastic, a prop stashed in the trunk. It's a theater, after all. But when those bones rubbed against my skin, it was like touching sandpaper, and I reconsidered my assumption. Ugh." Ruby shuddered and wrapped her arms around herself.

Jeremy fought the urge to hold her, comfort her.

For a full minute Ruby stood rooted to the spot before she squared her shoulders. "Let's look through the costumes, see if we can figure out their attraction."

Ruby moved to the back of the room and thumbed through hangers draped with colorful pantaloons, gowns complete with lightweight petticoats and, heaped in a pile on the floor, pairs of beaded shoes tapered to a curled point.

Jeremy frowned. "Shoes that befit a Genie. How many pairs?"

"Five, plus a single shoe. Think he took the other?"

"As a trophy? Maybe. You didn't see him carrying anything when he struggled with you, but they're small and pliable. He could have pocketed it."

"Or it may have gone missing years ago."

"Still, he took a chance. Instead of racing off, he stops to window-shop and you almost catch him."

"I agree, it doesn't make a lot of sense. Splayed

on the floor in the other room, I guess he thought I wasn't a threat, but he had to see me struggling to my feet when he ran." Ruby stroked her chin. "Why not make a clean getaway?"

Jeremy shrugged. "Because the opportunity to check for valuable gems overpowered our prowler's common sense."

Jeremy heard Ruby catch her breath and wondered if his reference to the prowler as "our" as opposed to "your" had crossed a line. He stepped backward to give her room.

Ruby turned to face him. "I think I've got everything here, and there's a potential witness to interview."

"Right, Lucille, that sweet little old lady." Jeremy smiled.

"Legend has it that sweet little old lady was less sugary back in the day."

"Then it should be interesting."

"Interesting? Maybe. But you need to remember, if people think some outsider wants to pry into their business, they'll clam right up, so your job is to stay in the background."

"Got it."

Ruby's dictum sounded harsh even to her own ears, but Jeremy's tendency to second-guess her and the other members of the team grated. True, the serial burglar continued to outwit her, and now she had to sort out the puzzle of the trunk full of bones, but she was convinced that in the fight against crime, hard work would prevail, and good would triumph over evil. This bedrock conviction had propelled her into the arena of public service, and in the three years since her election to office, events had born out her belief. Until now.

Her lack of progress in the serial burglary case chipped at her confidence. It didn't help that this final year of office demanded she divide her time between crime-busting and reelection activities, or that the city council saw fit to import extra help on the assumption she could not meet her mandate with the resources at hand.

Even more disconcerting was the mix of emotions Jeremy managed to awaken inside her each time he spoke. It had been five years since her husband's death, five years since the low timbre of a voice could spark excitement and awareness in her. Was there potential for a romantic relationship with Jeremy, or were her symptoms a reaction to her lackluster love life? She banished these thoughts as they walked the five hundred feet to Lucille's home.

"Give me a rundown on the house, please," Jeremy said as he stepped over a curb.

Ruby stopped for a moment. "It's an American Foursquare, named for its box structure, built mid-1890s to 1930. Some historians claim the simple style was meant to repudiate the more ornate architecture of the Victorians, which had dominated the previous sixty years. There are lots of them in Tinker west of the railway tracks, probably because they were an economical choice back in the day. What's your interest?"

"I wonder why a woman from a prominent family would choose to live in an American Foursquare instead of a structure more befitting her social status, such as a Victorian or a mountain rustic."

Ruby sighed. "I don't know. Maybe when I get through questioning Lucille, you can ask her."

Ruby raised her hand to knock on the front door. Lanterns, a door wreath and a straw Thanksgiving mat decorated the porch. *You may have a reputation as a gossip, but you do know how to decorate for a holiday.*

Lucille ushered them into a square room on the right. Here, the front of a formal dining area had been converted into a conversation alcove. A rose-petal teapot with matching cups and saucers surrounded a plate of oatmeal cookies on a mahogany coffee table. Ruby settled in one of the three wing chairs and took out her notebook to review the questions she intended to ask during the interview. But before she had a chance to activate her audio recorder, Lucille blindsided everybody.

THREE

"I know who broke into my theater last night."
Lucille picked up a cookie and halved it with one
bite.

Ruby's "Who?" was almost drowned out by Jeremy's "How?" Ruby shot him a warning glance,
then pressed Record. After stating the date and
time and naming the speaker, Ruby repeated her
question.

"Who? Frank Dosser, that's who." Lucille
brushed the crumbs from her hands.

Dosser, a longtime local politician and the
current mayor, used the campaign slogan "Prosper with Dosser" to brand himself, though Ruby
couldn't recall any great improvement in Tinker's
economy since he'd held office. Still, she wondered how Frank had made it into Lucille's bad
books.

"Why do you think it was Frank?" Ruby's hand
wavered over the cookie plate.

"The way he moves. It's as plain as the hat on
your head."

"Care to explain?"

"Well, dearie, when Frank Dosser takes a step he wobbles ever so slightly, like a bowling ball balancing at the edge of the gutter. He probably walks on the outer edges of his feet, and if you look, I bet you'd find uneven wear patterns on his soles."

Ruby had never looked at the soles of Dosser's shoes; nor could she remember his gait, but then she usually saw him standing behind a podium or in front of a new development project while being interviewed by the press.

There. The cookie to the left looked to be slightly bigger. Ruby eased it off the plate. "And you saw this?"

"Last night."

"So it was you who called in the prowler. Why didn't you identify yourself?"

"I wanted you here fast to catch him in the act. I was afraid if you thought an old lady called, you'd be less inclined to hustle."

"Lucille, everyone gets the same treatment. No judgment, that's my rule." Ruby began to nibble the cookie.

"That's not how it used to be. Years of favoritism, differential treatment of offenders, irregularities of protocol… I give you full credit for cleaning up the sheriff's office, but you know how it is, old habits. Anyway, you made good time."

"There was no moon last night and the woods

surrounding the theater made it dark as pitch. How could you see anything?"

Lucille set down her teacup. "I'll show you." She shuffled across the room to a wooden desk, opened a drawer and withdrew a pair of binoculars. "I've got two pair, these and ones with night vision."

Ruby turned the binoculars over in her hand, then hefted them up to her eyes and aimed them toward the theater. "Wow. I can see the wood grain on the side of the building even though it's all the way across the road. Why do you need that much power?"

"I've been the president of the Greater Tinker Bird Watching Society ten years running. If you're going to do a job, I say do it right. I've got binoculars, a field guide, spotting scope and journals. I waited all day yesterday with high hopes of sighting the elusive northern saw-whet owl in the evening, but that was before Dosser's shenanigans ruined the opportunity."

Ruby thought if Lucille's lip stuck out much farther she'd be in danger of tripping over it. She handed the binoculars back. "Even with these, you couldn't see his face, correct?"

"Correct." Lucille sniffed. "He wore a ski mask. But I know it was him. The study of birds is a study of motion, and what it comes down to is this—I'm an expert."

"This bird-watching stuff fascinates me," Jeremy said, and rose to his feet.

Ruby frowned.

Lucille beamed. "Let me show you." She moved back to the desk.

Jeremy followed.

Ruby bit her lip but stayed silent.

Lucille rummaged around her desk, then extracted several journals and handed them to Jeremy, who took them and returned to his seat. He flipped through the pages, then flattened an open journal on the coffee table. "You keep detailed records. Date, time, temperature, even location when sighted. Why does it matter where the bird was when you saw it?"

"I can tell you're a novice." Lucille's eyes twinkled. "Let's say I see a Swainson's hawk perched on the signpost overlooking the field out there. Since those birds prefer to position themselves on posts in grassy areas home to their food source, I can guess there's an infestation of caterpillars or grasshoppers on my property. The sighting isn't unusual. What would be odd is seeing one here in October, since they migrate south in large flocks by late August."

"You're saying bird-watchers track trends," Ruby said, cutting off Lucille from continuing the lecture.

"Yes."

Jeremy set down his teacup. "So, for example,

one way of telling if people were prowling around would be to note changes in bird traffic at a specific time of the day."

"Exactly right. I knew you were a smart one as soon as we met."

Jeremy puffed his chest ever so slightly and gazed at Ruby. She, in turn, looked at Lucille. "And are there any trends?" she asked.

"I could check through my ledgers and get back to you."

"Yes, please do." Ruby nodded, then pointed to the bottom of the journal page.

"At the bottom of your record, there is room for Comments. Did you make a notation about last night's prowler in your journal?"

"Oh yes. I noted the time of his arrival and of yours too."

"Good to know. Now here's the million-dollar question. Why would Dosser, or anyone for that matter, burgle the old theater?" Ruby leaned forward, hands empty, cookie eaten.

"I can't explain why bad guys do what they do. That's your job. I do know you don't need to prove motive to get a conviction in a real court. I watch television." Lucille patted her hair. "I also know the theater's been closed for decades, and prowlers haven't posed too much of a problem."

"But there have been occasions in the past?" Ruby wondered if the happy and sad masks hanging over the building's main entrance ever attracted unwanted attention.

"When it first closed, many considered the theater a bad omen. No one dared to go back inside. But with time, people forget. I remember once, seven years ago, a rumor circulated among the high school crowd about ghosts. They thought my old theater provided a likely home for the earthbound spirits. Someone heard about the ghost light and assumed I'd hung out a welcome sign.

"I put that notion to rest by giving them thorough tours of the grounds and the theater. They lost interest pretty quickly. Nothing drives away teens like older people who ramble on and on." Lucille winked.

"Do the props in the theater have any value?" Ruby reached for another cookie.

"Well, dearie, there aren't many props left in the theater. The brass fittings and sconces might attract a thief, and you'd only need a screwdriver to remove them, but I've never thought about them that way. And I've heard exit signs sold as vintage art deco pieces can be worth some money."

Lucille smiled, but the corners of her mouth turned down, as if some regret tinged the memories. "Lots of rhinestone jewels were sewn into costumes. The last production was supposed to be *Costume Party*, so a few stories may have circulated. But my parents would have removed anything of real value when the theater closed down.

As far as I know, those whispers never amounted to anything."

Ruby noticed the hesitation in Lucille's voice and raised her eyebrows. "Nothing?"

"Well, over the years people would volunteer to keep up the property by mowing the lawn and checking the building around this time of the year."

"You mean before Halloween," Ruby said.

"Yes. I always declined their offers."

"You had hired a maintenance man."

Lucille nodded. "I did. An older fellow who'd managed the apartments over on Culver Street before they were torn down to make way for those condos that launched Dosser's career. I can give you his name if you want to check him out."

"Thanks. So, the maintenance man is responsible for...?"

"Keeping up the grounds, cutting the lawn, maintaining the building, making sure the ghost light works—"

"Does he wash or wax the floors?" Ruby interrupted.

"He might. He sweeps the stage, the backstage and parts of the aisles not covered with rug. Why?"

"Officer Lawson slipped on the floor while walking down the aisle toward the stage. It seemed soapy. He could've hurt himself badly." Ruby noticed Jeremy flush but didn't let his embarrassment stop her. No one jeopardized any member of the team on her watch.

Lucille twisted a tissue in her hand. "Oh my, I'm glad no one was injured."

Ruby glanced at her watch. It was almost ten. "I've got a couple more questions. When and why did the theater close?"

Lucille chewed her lip.

Ruby sipped her tea and waited. She'd found the simple strategy worked. People often talked because silence made them uncomfortable.

Lucille shifted in her chair. Ruby still sat and hoped Jeremy could stop himself from speaking. No such luck.

He tapped the stack of journals in front of him. "I know you promised Ruby you'd look for trends, but is there any chance I could take some of these back to the station today?"

"How long would you need them?"

"Only a couple of weeks. I'd like one year's worth working backward from today and six months on each side of when the high school kids wanted to bust ghosts in the theater."

"That's a lot of journals, but for you, dearie, anything. Just let me get them."

Lucille began to rise from her chair.

Ruby cleared her throat. "Lucille, I still need to know about the theater closure."

"Oh yes, of course." Lucille sat back down and rested her hands in her lap. "Now, let me think.

It was a long time ago. I'll start with a bit of history. My parents owned the building and allowed a group of us who fancied ourselves actors to use the theater. We produced shows and made a small profit because people donated everything and everyone volunteered.

"We were extra excited about our last production, *Costume Party*, which had debuted to great success on Broadway in the fifties. How could we go wrong?" Lucille shrugged, opened her arms and spread her fingers wide.

"From the start, the whole thing seemed doomed. First, our order for a gong went awry. Next, our seamstress broke her hand, which delayed the opening for six weeks." Lucille clenched her fists. "You wouldn't believe the things… Anyway, the day before the theater closed for good, my best friend, Eleanor Costell, and I decided to run lines. We were sitting in the props room sharing Pixy Stix candy when she up and suggested we leave and go west."

"Her suggestion surprised you?"

"Oh, she'd spoken about the glamour of the West Coast before, but I'd always thought it was just talk. This time she insisted our production would never happen. She'd heard radio announcers telling of dozens of Hollywood directors looking for girls like us."

Ruby smiled. "You must have been excited."

"I couldn't believe my ears. It was one thing to

pretend we'd go pro, but I had a hard time believing she was serious. I argued that we couldn't do it, that we had too many ties to Tinker. Graduation was in two months. We'd both applied to colleges, and there was a good chance at least she'd be accepted. I had a steady boyfriend and Harvey was sweet on her. Then there was the shock to our families."

"Did you persuade her?"

"Eleanor heard me out. She didn't disagree with me, and I thought that would be the end of it. We started to practice our lines."

"What happened next?" Ruby prompted.

Lucille clasped her arms around herself in a body hug, then exhaled noisily. "Billy Jenkins happened next. He was to play the hero, but his mother forbade him from continuing with our production, something about a feud with Anna Jones's mother. Anna was to play opposite him. He burst into the prop room to tell me the news."

"You sound upset."

Lucille gazed into space. "You'd think after all this time the memory wouldn't be as fresh, but telling it makes it seem like yesterday. As if we didn't have enough drama, to try to cast someone else in the role would be almost impossible, and the news couldn't have come at a worse time."

Lucille began to wring her hands. "With Eleanor suggesting we chuck everything and leave town and Billy pulling out of the show, I was in a bad position."

"What did you do?" Ruby asked.

"I took Billy outside to calm him down. When I came back, Eleanor had gone. That evening, she didn't go home, and her disappearance became a source of worry. I told the sheriff what I knew, and after a short investigation, they concluded she'd left for Hollywood on her own."

"Did anyone besides Billy Jenkins go into the theater that last day?"

Lucille frowned. "These are the same questions the sheriff asked me over fifty years ago, and I'll give the same answers. I don't know. They could have. If there wasn't a scheduled event, any of the volunteers or actors might drop in, but I can tell you that when I returned after talking to Billy, the theater was empty and everything was cleaned up and in its place, save for the Pixy Stix we'd been eating. She'd even taken both scripts with her."

Now Ruby frowned. "I still don't understand why Eleanor's disappearance would cause the theater to close."

"A lot of people thought the theater jinxed us. The core group of actors refused to continue with *Costume Party* or any other production unless we selected a new venue for shows."

"Did you believe the venue caused the problems?"

"No, but I was hurt Eleanor left without saying goodbye. I lost my taste for acting. Walking through the theater door depressed me. Even though my parents shut it down and refurbished the old movie house on Main, I didn't eat or sleep well for months."

"You don't suspect the maintenance man is the burglar, do you?" Jeremy looked at Ruby quizzically as they walked toward the car.

"No. Why would the maintenance man, who has access to the theater twenty-four-seven, break in to it last night and risk arrest? If he wanted to take something, he could do that on his rounds."

"True. Did you believe her story?"

Ruby considered a moment. "Not completely, no, but her story shouldn't be too difficult to double-check. Apparently it satisfied the sheriff then. One thing's for sure. Unless there were other people who disappeared at the time, it's very likely the skeletal remains are Eleanor Costell."

FOUR

It seemed ludicrous in light of today's standards, but Ruby could understand how people would accept the story that someone had disappeared fifty years ago, driven by dreams of Hollywood stardom. Against the backdrop of the late sixties, a time of hitchhikers and hippies, Janis Joplin and Tiny Tim, social upheaval became the norm, and thousands of young people migrated to hot spots such as Haight-Ashbury. Who was to say the heady atmosphere wouldn't attract a girl from Tinker?

What next? A review of the police records and old newspaper accounts was a place to start. She also planned to call the forensic anthropologist before the end of the day.

"Mind if I drive back to the office?" Jeremy placed the volumes of bird journals on the back seat of the car.

Startled out of her reverie, Ruby considered his request. She disliked relinquishing control and rarely accepted the role of passenger in any motor vehicle. "I drove the car here," she stated.

"But each one is part of a small fleet established for all the officers to use," Jeremy said.

Although the car felt like hers, she had to admit he was technically correct. Any officer could use any available car. She rocked back and forth, heel to toe, while she considered his suggestion.

"If I drive, it'll help familiarize me with the territory."

True, it would. Still she hesitated. Ruby knew it was a stereotype, but he was from New York City, where drivers had a reputation of being rage-filled and reckless, not that there would be much traffic on the road today.

"I know what you're thinking," Jeremy said. "You don't trust my driving, but a study conducted in 2021 ranked New York drivers the safest when the fifty states were compared. Colorado drivers only scored in the middle of the pack. I took a chance on your driving this morning; now it's your turn." He grinned.

Ruby disguised her eye roll with a cough.

Torn between standing her ground and giving in, she frowned. He'd used his charm to butter up Lucille. Now he had her in his sights. She vowed to shore up her defenses. "We're talking about one simple car ride," Jeremy said, "not racing in the Indy 500."

She prided herself on being decisive, yet here

she was, continuing to tread water. Jeremy's eagerness, brown eyes wide as he stared at her with rapt attention, was appealing. Besides, an advantage of letting Jeremy drive would be the opportunity for her to continue to mentally organize a to-do list based on Lucille's statement and the evidence they'd collected at the theater.

"All right," she said at last. Ruby handed Jeremy the keys, then moved to the passenger side of the car.

Jeremy settled behind the steering wheel and inhaled. The pine-scented air invigorated him, and he left his window partially open despite the November chill. He looked sideways. Ruby had fastened her seat belt and relaxed into her seat. *That's a good sign.*

He levered the seat back to provide more leg room, turned the key and pressed down on the gas pedal. Ruby sat straighter and began fiddling with the air vents. He wondered why any adjustments were necessary if she'd originally set the car to her preferences.

"Anywhere you need to go before we head back to the station?" He hoped she'd suggest a favorite restaurant for takeout. He'd only had toast and coffee for breakfast. "First day on the job" nerves had killed his appetite earlier, but now his stomach had resumed squawking.

"Thanks, I'm good."

When they passed a hamburger drive-through with its airborne aroma of charbroiled food, his mouth watered, but Jeremy kept his eyes on the road.

A sign warned of a four-way intersection ahead. As Jeremy slowed the car, Ruby opened the glove compartment and began to rifle through the papers inside. The rustling distracted him. He clenched his hands on the wheel as Ruby pulled out a wad of pages and began to sort them on her lap. "Do you need me to pull over so you can go through those?"

"Nope, I've got this." Ruby continued to shuffle and stack the papers.

Jeremy clenched his jaw. The rustling made his skin prickle. But as he drove through the intersection, Ruby realigned the documents and returned them to the glove compartment.

He increased his speed but stayed below the posted limit. Why couldn't Ruby relax and enjoy the ride? He could see her hands balled into fists so tight her knuckles were white. He decided to try talking about the case, but Ruby only uttered a few noncommittal replies to his questions. When he changed course and began talking about how he was adjusting to Tinker, Ruby turned her head away, gazed out the window and said nothing.

Finally he gave up any attempt at conversation, turned left onto Ponderosa Avenue and groaned. Fast food alley straight ahead. The sight of the signs advertising everything from fried chicken to submarine sandwiches overrode protocol. He turned into the lot of the submarine shop.

"Sorry, but I'm famished."

Ruby merely nodded.

While Jeremy lined up to order, Ruby greeted an elderly couple, then spoke to a group of men commandeering the tables by the windows. *She talks to everyone but me. What's with that?*

He paid for his food and walked over to join her. But instead of waiting there to introduce him, she finished her conversation, intercepted him, and together they walked back to the car.

"Want a cookie?" He held out a double chocolate chip.

"No thanks."

Jeremy finished his meal and started the car. "I'm fueled up and ready to go. It should be clear sailing back to the office, straight down Ponderosa to Pine Ridge Road."

Another five minutes and the difficult ride would be over. He could hardly wait. As they approached a curve, Ruby yelled, "Watch out!"

Jeremy jumped and tromped the brakes. The car squealed to a stop. "What now?"

"Over there." Ruby pointed across the road where a rabbit was hesitating to run. "It was about to jump onto the road. It startled me."

Jeremy felt his patience evaporating, but he said nothing.

"That was bad, wasn't it?" Ruby hung her head a moment. "I'm sorry. I don't know what's gotten into me."

"This isn't working," Jeremy admitted. They'd driven less than ten miles, starting and stopping, doing anything and everything but communicating, but at least he'd gotten lunch. "Wanna change seats?"

"Yes, please."

Jeremy unbuckled his seat belt. Ruby did the same.

"So much for familiarizing myself with Tinker."

"I thought I could let someone else do the driving. Guess it's just not in me."

Jeremy recognized a sinking in the pit of his stomach. What bothered him wasn't the reduced opportunity to drive; it was the realization that the sheriff had an issue about control, which reminded him of the difficulties in New York that led to his transfer to Tinker. He could only hope this new experience wouldn't mirror his career trajectory of the past.

For a minute or two, they drove east around Casper Lake until Ruby pulled onto the shoulder and let the car idle. She pointed to the body of water.

"Looks calm, doesn't it?"

"Oh, yeah."

"I used to spend time here as a young girl. It seemed so big I thought this was an ocean. But calm can be deceptive. Casper Lake empties into Casper River, which becomes Casper Rapids, then yonder, around the corner, you get the Casper Waterfall."

"Any fish in the lake?"

"Some. Once the sheets of ice thicken to four inches, people put up huts. You can expect to land some trout, bass, crappie. And in the spring, once the ice melts, a lot of people fly-fish. Huh. Listen to me, I sound like a tourist guide."

"Do you fish?"

"Used to." Ruby smiled.

"Me too." Jeremy smiled back at her, pleased her memories had created this lighter mood. During the remainder of the drive, the silence was more comfortable.

Ruby parked at the station, then walked around to the back of the patrol car. Jeremy had almost reached the front door of the office when a reporter and cameraman ran a pincer movement and positioned themselves between him and the sheriff. When he turned he saw the same perspective as the television team. Ruby, only thirty feet away, faced the news media alone.

After she fielded and answered questions for several minutes, the reporter summarized. "So on October 18, a call about a prowler inside the old Grand Theater brought you out to investigate. You also confirmed pursuing an intruder. Unfortunately this intruder escaped. You are not sure if this is the same person responsible for the string of burglaries that have plagued Tinker over three months, but what is becoming clear is something else, more puzzling, also occurred at the theater that night. Care to explain further, Sheriff?"

If the reporter's question surprised Ruby, she didn't show it. There were no tells in her relaxed stance or steady gaze.

"While in the process of chasing said prowler, I found a human skeleton. We are in the process of collecting evidence in order to identify the bones and determine, if possible, the cause of death. I'll have more information as the investigation proceeds."

"Do you think the prowler is connected to the skeleton?"

"I can't say at this time."

Ruby smiled and started to move toward the office, but the reporter blocked her path and thrust the microphone closer to her face.

"You are the first female sheriff of Tinker, Colorado. There are those who argue that the pressure of this job isn't for everyone. Do you think the unsolved burglaries, the prowler you let escape and the newfound bones will affect the public's confidence in your continued ability to do the work?"

"Let me be clear. The prowler did escape, but

I did not let them escape. On the contrary, I did everything in my power to prevent their escape."

"You don't think your failure to make an arrest will provide fodder for the naysayers and impact your election chances?"

Ruby frowned and pushed her hat back. "No, I don't. I believe the majority of people in Tinker have confidence in me and my ability to close cases. I know I am able to do the work and to get reelected. My job includes everything from sorting out misunderstandings through working on more complex cases to chasing bad guys. I bring criminals to justice. Some cases take longer to resolve than others, but I'm proud of my closure rate."

"So can we expect an arrest of the serial burglar who has been holding the businesses of Tinker hostage?"

"Yes. Policing can be difficult and time-consuming, and I'd love to have immediate answers for the public. But we need to gather and examine the evidence. This takes time. However, I can assure everyone that there will be an arrest, and soon."

"One last question. Mayor Frank Dosser has gone on record saying there's an exciting new crime fighter in town. Do you share his sentiment?"

Ruby bowed her head for a moment, then looked directly at the camera. "I'm always grateful for any assistance in the fight against crime. That's all for now, thank you."

Ruby strode past the reporter and cameraman, past him and into the office.

Jeremy watched the news team pack up and leave, then went inside. "Wow. You were really cool out there. If I were in your shoes, I might have lost it."

Ruby smiled, but it didn't reach her eyes, and the ends of her mouth remained turned down. "A part of the job is to handle communication with the people of Tinker. Sometimes I wonder if Bess Trundle—that's the reporter, by the way—purposely baits me. But then I figure if she wonders about something, a bunch of people in the viewing audience will wonder about the same thing. Best to keep your hackles down and put their minds at ease."

But Jeremy couldn't stop himself from worrying. Bad memories of confrontational media still burned bright. An ugly scene had played out when a reporter contended Jeremy had targeted someone as a suspect in an armed robbery, someone who had criticized and harangued him at every turn. The allegation wasn't true. He'd followed the evidence, calculated the probabilities and produced a profile, as he'd done a hundred times in the past.

First one reporter, then many reporters argued that Jeremy, the "golden boy" of criminology, had torpedoed his nemesis so he could slide off the hot seat and secure bigger and better promotions.

It wasn't true. His profile provided general parameters, but no one had believed Jeremy when he argued that the way it had been applied could be at fault.

It didn't help that indignation and anger fueled his reactions to the allegations of impropriety. He looked guilty. He sounded guilty. He began to wonder if he was guilty.

His self-doubt vanished when the police used his profile to make an arrest and convince the grand jury to bring an indictment. But in the end, the suspect won an acquittal and sued for false imprisonment, and his newfound confidence evaporated while his career plummeted.

He felt isolated and alone. He had grown up with God; believed in His protection without question. But the career crisis had put a barrier between them. And he had a sinking feeling that the transfer to the small Colorado town was a demotion. But his supervisor had a connection with a commissioner in Tinker, and Tinker was having a problem with crime.

He hadn't wanted to leave at first, but then he realized—or hoped—his skill and prior good record as a cop had fueled his boss's decision to loan him to this department. He recalled the conversation when he was ordered to report to Tinker within a week for assignment.

"Can't I redeem myself here?"

"We've got to calm things down, son," his supervisor had said. "They need you in Tinker. We'll handle the press from our end, and in four months you'll be back with us. You'll see."

Was this his path to redemption? As he'd driven to Tinker, he'd decided God had handed him a second chance.

He could guess that Ruby knew nothing about his fall from grace, but he couldn't shake a feeling of unease. If information about his alleged mistake became public knowledge, would it affect her opinion of him? And why did he care so much?

FIVE

"Okay, people, come one, come all." Deputies Desmond Martinez, Bill Kirk and Deborah Dean gathered round Ruby. "You too, Jeremy."

His stomach tightened. *What now?*

The sight of everyone settling in with their lunches sent a shock wave through him. He'd missed the memo about the meet and munch session, obviously a Monday afternoon tradition, and covered by making a mug of tea to bring to the table.

"Welcome to the weekly roundup," Ruby began. "Most of you have met Jeremy Lawson. It may be old news, but he's been assigned to the team temporarily, so he'll be sticking with me for the duration of his stay. If he needs any help, well, you know the drill."

The deputies nodded.

"Most of you also know I discovered a skeleton last night. The state's forensic anthropologist just called me with her preliminary finding. Due to the nature of injuries on the skull, she's calling it a homicide, which means we've got a very old murder on our plate. This, in addition to the serial burglaries, will demand most of my attention. All remaining deputies are to keep their focus on maintaining community peace."

"And that's my entrée," Bill said. "Let's see. Last week was pretty quiet except for our usual arrest for drunkenness in a public place."

"Jeb Hancock, right?" Desmond asked.

"Correct. This time I handled him personally. All through the booking process, he kept mumbling about looking forward to good old biscuits with sausage gravy and eggs for breakfast."

Desmond laughed and looked at Jeremy. "Ever since Mrs. Hancock died and we changed our cook, he's become a regular guest. Hancock's harmless enough, but I think he aims to get arrested. Maybe someone should give him cooking lessons."

"It'd keep him out of our hair," Ruby agreed. "You volunteering?"

"Me? No." Desmond grinned. "I barely boil water, but Mrs. Sandberg, now there's a woman who can cook up a storm. And since Mr. Sandberg met his demise, she's got no one to feed and fuss over."

"Right. We'll just rename ourselves Sheriff's Office and Matchmakers Central, see what Bess Trundle thinks of that. Still—" Ruby scratched her head "—it's not too terrible an idea."

Bill looked down at his notes. "Speaking of Mrs. Sandberg, she complained about her ghost again. Keeps hearing thumping in her attic."

"Noisy fella, huh?" Deborah wagged her finger. "Now Desmond, this one's for you. Get a cage from animal control and go over to Mrs. Sandberg's. While you're capturing the 'ghost,' plant some seeds about how Jeb needs care and comfort, being as he's all by his lonesome."

"Worth a try," Desmond agreed. "I'll get on it."

Ruby looked at Jeremy. "Guess you're starting to see policing in Tinker is a far cry from the action-packed life you've led in the big city."

"It's a change." Jeremy didn't mention that a bulk of his time had been spent in a cubicle analyzing numbers and looking for trends, like thousands of other office workers.

"Oh, I almost forgot," Bill said. "Man came in from over Bugle way, trying to sell us computer gizmos, soft something. I listened as long as I could, but he was speaking a foreign language. Finally got rid of him by taking a card." He pulled a standard business card out of his pocket and tossed it on the table.

Jeremy perked up. "Anyone mind?" When nobody objected, he grabbed it, turning it over in his hand.

Black lettering on white business stock in easy-to-read Times New Roman font, a contact phone number, and a short list of software products attracted him like a dog to a bone. He read aloud: "C-U-P, P-A-N, G-E-G. Wow, this guy has top-of-the-line stuff. The CUP, for example, would enable us to access the location of habitual sex offenders. PAN data-mines."

"Data what?" Deborah cupped a hand behind her ear as if she'd misheard him.

"Data-mines. You input parameters to get data sets which you can analyze for useful information. There are even programs for geographic profiling."

"Which will do what for us, exactly?" Ruby raised her eyebrows.

"If we mark the spots on a map of each of our burglaries we might find they cluster around a geographic area. There's a theory that bad guys prefer familiar areas where they know the territory, places where they live or work. It can point us in a certain direction when we look for this guy."

Bill waved his hand. "But can't you tape a map to a wall and use pushpins to do it yourself, without a computer program?"

"In some cases, yes, but these programs let you access larger quantities of information faster. It's like comparing writing a novel by using a manual typewriter instead of a computer. Look, I understand the office may not be able to afford software upgrades, but could I at least meet with this guy?"

"We already liaison with Denver for stuff like DNA comparisons using CODIS." Bill shrugged.

"We sent our bones off to the forensic anthropologist in Denver because we don't have enough work to employ any such person here full-or even part-time," Ruby added.

"I get that, but a meeting will give me an idea of what's out there if and when there's room in the budget for even one purchase."

Ruby laughed. "You know what they say, no harm in looking. Just don't get too excited. We're Tinkerites, which means we prefer more traditional methods of investigation, like talking to each other face-to-face instead of crunching numbers or compiling whatever these computer programs collect."

"Got it."

As the meeting dispersed, Jeremy congratulated himself. He might not wear a cowboy hat like everybody else, but winning even a bit of the technological round gave him a foothold.

He realized he needed to be accepted as part of this caring team geared toward promoting community, which was a world away from being behind the scenes in a unit focused on a war on crime.

With any luck, he'd be able to usher the sheriff's office into the modern world. All it would take would be to familiarize one person with a software program, and before you knew it, everyone would be on board.

* * *

Ruby smiled at the memory of Jeremy's facial expression by the end of the weekly meet and munch. She couldn't deny the change in his comfort level as the conversation moved to technological gadgetry. His tension dissipated; the cords in his neck relaxed, and his color improved. She and him. Could two people in law enforcement be any different? Could they ever work together as a team, or was Jeremy just another weight around her neck, someone else she was obligated to look out for?

She decided to try brainstorming with him, so she cleared a space on her desk, pulled out the weekly organizing charts, and placed them on top of two spreadsheets, one titled Burglaries, the other titled Murder, and then buzzed Jeremy on the intercom.

Ruby looked up from her desk when Jeremy walked through the door. His dark tousled hair, swarthy complexion and five o'clock shadow at three in the afternoon made her breath hitch. His warm smile temporarily banished her worry about her unsolved cases. Her heart wondered how a date with him would look, but her head overruled the impulse. She had been widowed almost four years, but the thought of going on an official date made her head spin and her heart ache. Besides, she didn't mix business with pleasure.

After he sat down, she began to speak. "I mentioned at the roundup that we have confirmation of a homicide. When I spoke to the forensic anthropologist, my end of the conversation consisted of telling her we have anecdotal evidence pointing to Eleanor Costell as the victim."

"What about DNA?" Jeremy asked.

Ruby hated getting interrupted and squelched a rush of annoyance. "To get a DNA match, don't you need to make a comparison? Even if the anthropologist gets a sample from the bones, there's nothing of Eleanor's for an evaluation. DNA was not collected back in the forties. Plus she was an only child with no known relatives other than her parents, who died over twenty years ago, which rules out the possibility of any forensic genealogy analysis."

"That answers my question. But maybe the forensic anthropologist can complete a digital facial reconstruction, if the bones aren't too far gone."

"I'm sure if she can, she will, Jeremy. The bones are sitting in Denver, after all, and they have a full complement of investigative tools. In the meantime, if we can determine the day of death was near the date of the theater closure, a search of the police records and newspaper archives might divulge if anyone else disappeared during the same time frame."

"More circumstantial evidence." Jeremy sighed.

"Circumstantial is a start. I plan to visit Tinker Dental after this meeting. They took over when

Dr. Hooker retired. I'm hoping his old records will include information about Eleanor, which I can send to Denver."

"If they go back that far."

"Always the optimist," Ruby muttered.

Jeremy gazed out the window.

"So, let's list the names of key players in both cases." Ruby selected a marker and turned to the whiteboard behind her desk. She'd asked Bill to retrieve it from the records room, and he'd not only set it up in here but cleaned it off too.

"You know, they have digital whiteboards on the market now."

Ruby turned back to look at Jeremy. "Oh?"

"Yeah, a digital whiteboard has lots of tools and functions. You can browse the net and run timed exercises. They're supposed to increase focus and creativity."

"Are you having trouble focusing, Jeremy?"

"No, of course not, I was just saying."

She wrote *Frank Dosser* down in the Burglar category.

"On the basis of Lucille's say-so? Seems weak." Jeremy's mouth turned down and he seemed to deflate.

Ruby couldn't tell whether he was reacting to her dismissal of his digital whiteboard suggestion or her acceptance of part of Lucille's statement. She thought about offering him some sort of concession, then changed her mind. She needed to stay focused on the case, or cases. Her future depended on it.

"I said earlier I didn't buy everything she was selling, but I do think she pays extra attention to detail, a necessary trait for a gossip. And remember, you thought enough of her observations to leave with her bird ledgers."

"Okay, okay. Frank makes the grade. Anyone else a suspect in the burglaries?"

"We'll discuss that later. I want to finish with Lucille's statement first."

Jeremy thought a moment. "Based on Lucille's statement, I think we should add Billy Jenkins and Anna Jones to the list of murder suspects."

"Forget Jenkins. He was killed in a car crash over twenty years ago."

"That's unfortunate. He won't be able to substantiate Lucille's alibi. But if Lucille is telling the truth, he did leave with her initially. After their discussion, she headed back into the theater but left without seeing Eleanor. Then Billy could have returned to the theater, gotten in an argument with Eleanor and killed her. I think we should include him. No one said the murderer is still living."

"Good point." Ruby wrote *Billy Jenkins* and *Anna Jones* on the whiteboard, then pointed to Anna's name. "Think we can make a murderer out of her?"

"Rivalry between actors? A dispute over a boy? You never know what we'll find out."

Ruby read the three names aloud and pinched her lips. "It's pretty paltry."

"I've got one more to add. Lucille."

Ruby sighed. "I haven't added her mostly because I don't much like her."

Jeremy raised his eyebrows.

"I know it sounds illogical. But when I was eight years old I had a classmate. One of the in crowd. She had everything—good looks, great clothes and a family with money. There were rumors she cheated to get good grades, rumors I never doubted. And she'd tease me. I hated her and wished she'd go away."

"We've all had those feelings when we were kids."

"Anyway, one day my wish came true. She did go away. At first, I was overjoyed. But a few days turned into a week. Then I learned she'd had an accident on her bike. Ended up in the hospital for months."

"Yikes."

"Talk about guilt. I was sure my wish had contributed to or maybe even caused her accident. Fast-forward to today. I take it very slow when I deal with someone I dislike. No hasty judgments, no secret wishes."

"I understand how you feel." Jeremy rested his arms on his legs. "I find Lucille charming, but I can give you lots of reasons to list her as a suspect. First, we only have her word about what happened the day before Eleanor disappeared. At the very least, we have to check the story. Will other people verify that Eleanor talked about leaving for Hollywood? Did anyone see Billy Jenkins leave the theater with Lucille? The fact that I find her delightful may speak more to my lack of experience with people than to any great power of perception."

"Your arguments are heard and accepted." Ruby added *Lucille* to the whiteboard. "So, three people, but we may have to add more as we unearth additional information about the victim."

"Affirmative. Do you think the prowler at the theater and the murderer are connected?"

Ruby took off her hat, set it on her desk, and patted down her hair. "No, I don't. I'm sure I've got two separate cases. If the burglar and the murderer are one and the same, that puts them in their late seventies or older. The person I wrestled with last night was no octogenarian."

"What about the burglaries?"

"I'm not sure if the burglar at the theater is the same person who committed the burglaries over the past three months, but a number of similarities about the crimes including the time they occurred, the type of venue chosen, and the fact valuable property was left on the premises suggest we're looking for one perp. Of course I may be in denial. If the burglaries aren't committed by the same person, that gives me three separate crimes. Ugh."

"If they are separate crimes, you'd have to ask yourself why someone would suddenly be interested in poking around the old theater after how many years?"

"You're right." Ruby nodded. "I'll put checking out new rumors about the theater on our follow-up list. But I still haven't been able to compile much of a suspect list, which may be why the commissioners decided to call in extra help."

"That would be me." Jeremy grinned.

"Yes, indeed." Ruby stopped herself from smiling. "I did have a couple people of interest on my radar, but with no evidence to connect them to any of the crime scenes, my inquiries hit a dead end. Facts need to be compiled, and I understand you've been called into Tinker for that purpose, but right now I'd rather us focus on the homicide."

"Right. The autopsy report will need to be considered when we examine the photographs taken at the theater, and the physical evidence should be sorted. We could convert the records room into an incident room. Grab the whiteboard. I'll set up a table and spread out what we've got." Jeremy paused and his voice trailed off. "Have I overstepped my boundaries?"

Ruby scowled. "Not really." Her voice sounded tart, even to herself. Nothing he'd said was incorrect or out of line, but behind the scenes, Jeremy issued marching orders like a general about to do battle. Would he be as bossy if paired with a man, or was she overreacting, becoming too sensitive?

"Should we get started now?" Ever the eager beaver, Jeremy began to move.

But before she could say anything, Ruby heard a bang in the front office. She bolted upright so quickly her chair shot out from under her, and she slammed her hip into the side of the desk as she pushed past Jeremy and rushed out the door.

When she looked into the front office she saw Mayor Frank Dosser at the counter, reddened face, narrowed eyes and bared teeth. And then he started to holler.

SIX

"There you are!" The mayor pointed at Ruby. "You need to act and I mean right now. If Lucille Trefor isn't stopped, so help me, I'll do something that'll shut her jabbering mouth permanently."

"Now, Frank."

"Don't you 'now, Frank' me, Sheriff. Your career's not going down in flames. But if she keeps saying what she's saying, I'll be ruined." He accentuated his speech by pounding his fist on the counter.

"What's she saying?"

"That I'm some sort of suspect in a burglary. At the theater. Maybe even in a string of burglaries." He spat out the words.

Ruby sensed Jeremy coming to stand beside her. To prevent him interfering in her battle, she put her hand on his arm.

"What would you like me to do, Frank?"

"Shoot her in the knee."

"I can't do that."

"Then give me your gun and I'll do it. She'd be

so busy paying attention to her own pain, she'd forget to be one."

Ruby struggled not to smile.

"It's not funny. I'm serious. Do you know how fickle the voting public can be?"

"You forget, Frank, I'm elected too."

"Yeah, I guess you are. Oh, hey, I get it. You're sore at me."

"Me? Why would I be sore?"

Frank's voice took on a placating tone. "When I asked that reporter—what's her name? Bess, that's it—if there was room in policing for females, she twisted my question into a negative statement. But I only posed the question, which I would have answered with a resounding *yes* if I'd had the chance."

"Really?"

"Really. Do you believe even for a moment I'd be foolish enough to challenge the competency of any worker by referring to their gender? That's worse than poor politics. It's suicide if you're running for office, even in a backwater like Tinker." Frank's face instantly reddened. "See, I did it again. I called our great town a backwater, which some people might find insulting. All I mean is Tinker isn't a radical hotbed."

"I understand, Frank. You're overwrought, so you're misspeaking. Don't worry. This is the sheriff's office, not a political debate or campaign rally. You're among friends." Ruby smiled.

"And about that other thing, when I described that new fella as exciting, I didn't mean to suggest he could overshadow you. I meant I was excited about adding an additional worker to the force. You agreed with me on that one."

"Yes, I did, and on the record too."

"That makes us good, right? Of course, right. So I repeat, you've got to do something about Lucille."

"I'm not sure my intervention is the wisest course of action, Frank. Think about it. Most people take Lucille Trefor with a large grain of salt. But if you react, by yourself or through me, it draws more attention to her stories. People may begin to think there's some truth in what she says."

"Hmm. You might have something there."

"And I can't say you're not a suspect in the burglary because most everyone is a suspect in the burglaries, including you."

"That's outrageous." Frank's face purpled. "We're back to where we started." Then he stood still for a moment. "I've got it. We can resolve this thing once and for all. I need to go to my car."

Frank turned on his heel, marched to his vehicle and flung the door open. He leaned over, opened the glove compartment and extracted what appeared to be an address book. When he turned and strode back, Ruby continued to watch his gait. She had to give credit to Lucille. Whether marching or striding, Frank moved like a bowling ball balanced on the edge of a gutter.

Thwap. The address book hit the counter with enough force to cause the penholder to vibrate. "I can prove where I was each time there was a burglary. My calendar will tell the tale."

Ruby grinned. "Great. You can give Officer Lawson your statement. If it checks out, you'll be crossed off the suspect list."

"I do that, and you'll announce I'm not a suspect?"

"I will indeed."

Satisfied, Frank moved behind the counter.

Ruby looked at the deputies, who remained in the front office. "After I visit Tinker Dental, I'll head home for the day," she told them, and she walked out the front door.

Jeremy stretched. He could transcribe Frank's statement tomorrow. Right now, a plate of spaghetti with olive oil and fresh garlic and a side of Broccolini called his name. He'd spotted a restaurant early this morning. The Red Raisin, Fine Italian Dining, the sign advertised. He smacked his lips and zipped up his jacket.

"Hang on there, Jeremy." Bill rose from his chair. "Before you go." He handed Jeremy a bundle which included paper, a five-by-seven notebook with lined paper, a pen and pencil, a pamphlet entitled Welcome to Tinker, and a map.

"Every transplant gets this orientation material from the Visitor's Center, but when we dish it out to new personnel, we add a request that you make best friends with the map by driving around and drawing the streets to familiarize yourself with their layout."

"How many deputies are transplants?"

"Most of us. I'm from Denver originally. Joined their police force right after graduating the police academy, but my ex—she's an artist—wanted to be closer to nature, so we moved to Tinker. Been here five years."

"Any regrets?"

"At first I worried about losing seniority, but relocating did wonders for my blood pressure. You wouldn't know it right now, but calm and crime-free are the two words I'd use to describe this place."

"Are Deborah and Desmond from the big city too?"

"Desmond's local, Tinker born and raised, but Deborah's from Hawaii."

"She's a long way from home."

"It's quite a story, ask her sometime."

"I will." Jeremy stuffed the packet into his pocket. "But now it's time for some dinner."

The Red Raisin was crowded, but he couldn't walk away from the smells of tomato sauce and basil that hit him when he first entered the restaurant. After Jeremy was seated, he placed his order, dug the map out of his pocket and tried to focus. Three main streets ran northwest to southeast parallel to US Route 24, which formed the boundaries of Tinker. A beehive of smaller roads branched from along both sides of the main arteries, but any nuances in the network were lost on paper. Bill was right. Driving the roads would create a more lasting impression. He just needed to find the time to do it.

The wait for his dinner provided an opportunity for Jeremy to review his first day on the job. One thing was for sure. It had been long.

The initial meeting he'd had with the commissioner who intimated he would "take care of him" because of a promise made to his supervisor in New York put him on edge. What was with that?

But he smiled to himself at the memory of his first encounter with Sheriff Ruby Prescott. She was cute, with green eyes and a dimple on her left cheek that appeared when she smiled. Her voice, low, almost sultry, and her relaxed stance, arms by her sides, bespoke a quiet confidence.

In different circumstances he'd follow up on his attraction. But her status as his boss, despite what the commissioner had said, caused him to shoot down any romantic inclination.

He poured water from a jug into his glass and sighed as the liquid sloshed over the side. Overcoming clumsiness was a forever goal. And how about his tendency to misstep whenever he tried to impress a woman? Because despite good intentions, he'd gotten off on the wrong foot with Ruby.

Getting caught ferreting through files made for a poor introduction. Jeremy tried to redeem himself by being conciliatory when confronted with the basics offered at the sheriff's office. But when he and Ruby collected evidence at the theater, his suggestions fizzled like wet firecrackers.

He gave himself a star for chatting with Lucille about bird-watching, but his attempt to drive the car back to the station showed misplaced intent, not good sense. What was he thinking, engaging in a debate over control of a vehicle?

And the results of his contributions to the weekly roundup totaled zero. Despite his best efforts, his bent toward technology could have made it appear that he believed himself to be superior to his coworkers.

But the day wasn't all bad. He'd enjoyed dipping his toes into the interviewing game when he took Dosser's statement. And Bill addressed him with respect in spite of their obvious differences of opinion regarding the use of software programs.

Jeremy wanted to become an integral member of the group for the duration of his stay in Tinker. Being part of God's team was important too. He needed to find a home church and made a mental note to ask one of the deputies about places of worship in Tinker.

He finished the meal, paid the check and then sat in his car and debated turning toward his apartment. Spending several hours in his rental didn't appeal to him. He hadn't set up his television. He didn't feel like staring at his laptop screen, and it was too early to go to bed. Although the sun had set forty minutes ago, there was sufficient street lighting to make familiarizing himself with the network of roads a realistic possibility. Perceptions of obstacles could change appreciably at different light levels. Now was as good a time as any to explore Tinker.

Decision made, Jeremy turned left onto Ponderosa Avenue, drove straight to the northernmost end of town and then stopped the car. He examined the map spread on the front passenger seat. Jeremy wondered whether the small cul-de-sacs that branched off Ponderosa to the north and south were unique to Tinker or a common feature of mountain towns.

Jeremy restarted the vehicle and slowly crisscrossed Ponderosa to check each side street for hidden entrances or back alleys. There were none. Heavy forest formed a barricade to hem in fenced backyards, leaving no room for even a footpath. He rated Bill's suggestion that he drive the streets to commit them to memory as excellent. Of particular interest were the moonlit shadows cast by small sheds and other outbuildings favored by homeowners.

As he reached the halfway point in the exercise, he noticed more homeowners shutting down for the night despite it being only 10:00 p.m., early by his standards. Landscape lights focused on front garden displays and porch lights located beside doorways winked out, leaving the darkness pierced only by beams from streetlamps.

Large rock formations jutted skyward north of Cumber Way, one of the few roads that continued to a smaller road named Pike's Pass. Its endpoint, Rock Garden Park, caught Jeremy's eye.

It was closed, of course. The elongated metal triangular gates blocked the entrance to traffic, so Jeremy shut down the engine and approached the gate on foot. He could just make out the corner of a building identified as the Trading Post to his right. A paved road curved through forested hills; rock faces extended as far as the eye could see.

Natural beauty assaulted him, more overpowering because the lack of color left only formidable shapes to stimulate his imagination. Cliffs and crags suggested strength and eternity and filled him with wonder. He looked up at the clouds and down at the earth and wondered if all the beauty that lay before him didn't prove the existence of a higher power. His faith had always been a cornerstone of how he perceived the world.

But what was his place in this picture? Did he even belong? He dropped his shoulders and ran his hands over his face. It was as if he'd been a particle of sand blown along a beach, never knowing where he'd land or why.

Was Tinker to be his doom or his destiny?

A *thunk* to his left interrupted his musing. If he scrunched his eyes, he could make out something splayed in the scrub grass no more than two feet from a pine tree. He stared hard. A large bird lay on its stomach with wings extended their full length, tips down. Its face wasn't visible, but Jeremy guessed it was the right body size for a bird of prey. He knew owls, hawks and even eagles were common throughout Colorado. Some surely called this place home.

He assumed park personnel would remove the carcass in the morning and was about to return to his car when it twitched. He didn't know what to do. He imagined Lucille could give him advice. Surely she'd seen and maybe even cared for injured birds. He pulled out his smartphone and scrolled down to her name. No answer. He opted not to leave a message.

In the office, he recalled seeing a notice about the county's animal control team and that it was available 24-7 for emergencies and started to search online for the number. Meanwhile, the bird jerked. There was no time to waste.

A reasonable compromise would be to keep trying animal enforcement while he investigated the extent of the creature's injuries himself. He could at least be a source of comfort while he waited for help to arrive.

Jeremy squatted, intending to climb through the widest part of the gap in the gate. He balanced on one foot and lifted the other, but the bird screeched, and Jeremy yelped and fell backward before regaining his balance. His heartbeat raced, a reaction to the emergency situation.

He needed to act now. He strode up to the gate and heaved his right leg over the top, but as he straddled it, a light flashed and an alarm shrilled. In less than a minute, a park security car pulled into the driveway, followed minutes later by an SUV marked Sheriff's Office. Jeremy exhaled noisily.

When Ruby stepped out of the car, he wondered how things could get any worse.

SEVEN

"Who do we have here?" Ruby's voice cut through the stillness and sent shock waves up Jeremy's spine.

He frowned and avoided her eyes. He gestured toward the spot where the bird lay, paused and craned his neck. His heart plummeted; the creature was gone. "I...there was a bird, injured."

Ruby moved beside him. "I don't see anything."

Jeremy pointed.

The park security officer peered through a pair of binoculars, then handed them to Ruby, who also aimed them at the spot Jeremy had indicated. "The bird has flown," she said, and pointed a finger as if to jab Jeremy in the chest.

"Why do you think we have security around this gate? Because we've had trouble with a vandal or vandals entering park premises after hours destroying property, that's why. Even with the best of intentions, simply going off the trails can disrupt and damage the environment."

"But—"

"No buts. Not to mention I'd gone to bed, so your actions not only endangered the park, they interrupted my sleep. Do you know how bad it looks to set a trap only to have it triggered by personnel associated with our office?"

"I couldn't help it."

"No? Your explanation had better be compelling."

Jeremy hoped it was, then launched into a description of what and why.

"And how did you plan to comfort an injured bird?" Ruby interrupted. "Stroke its feathers or maybe coo at it? Do you realize how silly that sounds?"

"'To serve and protect' is the mantra of law enforcement."

"But with provisos. Look, I saw the tamped-down grass. Based on its shape, the bird was likely a great horned owl. In colder climes like Colorado, these owls cache what they don't eat. When they return later, they warm the food by incubating it. What you thought was an injured bird was likely an owl 'cooking' its food."

"I had no idea."

"Yeah, well, you're a newbie round these parts. And I'll tell you something else. We call the great horned birds 'tiger owls' with good reason. They are not to be trifled with under any circumstance, especially if injured. Razor-sharp talons and a beak built for tearing combined with an aggressive personality add up to danger. Full stop."

Ruby sat in her car for a moment to regain her composure. Her head ached. The only consolation to this night's end was that a reporter hadn't shown up to capture Jeremy's embarrassing behavior or broadcast the ineptitude of the sheriff's office.

Until his arrival, she'd worked to keep the town of Tinker on an even keel and, for the most part, had succeeded. Now, not so much. Frustrated, Ruby pressed her head back against the seat.

Admittedly, she hated when things got out of whack. And if this latest escapade was any indication, few remedial actions remained. But there was nothing left to do tonight. Ruby took one last look at the starlit sky, then gripped the steering wheel and headed out.

Back home, she sat on the side of her bed. Her eyes fell on the photograph taken with two friends, all smiles as they stood with arms around one another outside a ski resort. Ruby felt blessed. Despite her husband passing, her life was getting back on track. She said a short prayer. *Things will improve tomorrow*, she told herself.

The next morning her phone pinged before she finished her eggs and toast. Although better than an emergency call, the request she swing by the town's municipal offices for an impromptu meeting with Commissioner Grant Grud caused a minor stomach upset.

Grant, a well-known moderate on hiatus from the law office bearing his name, combined his position as an elected official with an unfortunate interest in inflatable rafts. This led to rabble rousers opposed to his agenda shouting "put a pin in it" whenever he appeared at town halls. But Ruby liked him.

"Sit down, Sheriff. Make yourself comfortable."

Ruby took her hat off and smoothed her pants. She assessed Grant with a practiced eye. Aside from a platinum hair dye that clashed with his deep brown eyebrows and a flushed complexion Ruby suspected originated from a tight collar, he looked to be in good health.

Although some of the commissioners tried to inject themselves into the police process, Grant had a hands-off reputation, which made her wonder, *Why this meeting on this morning?* Grant bragged about his organizational skills, breadth of vision, and attention to detail. He didn't do impromptu. He also didn't keep Ruby waiting.

He reached into his jacket pocket, spread a letter on his desk and read the single sentence aloud. "It has come to my attention that Sheriff Ruby Prescott suppressed evidence at the scene of her husband's death." Grant patted the paper and looked Ruby in the eye. She stared at him dumbfounded.

"Found it under my door this morning."

Ruby fought back tears. A stab of pain seared her heart. "There's no truth to the allegation."

"I know that." Grant pressed his lips together. "So, who sent it and why?"

"We have to consider the timing." Ruby's voice broke and she swallowed hard before continuing. "It's common knowledge I'm running for reelection. Maybe someone wants to discredit me, either because they're angry or because they want to run for sheriff themselves."

"Got anyone in mind?"

Ruby paused before answering, "Not really. Maybe Tom Ewan, but this seems low even for him."

Grant chuckled. "If Tom got wind of any wrongdoing on your part, he'd never just send a letter."

"True." Ruby nodded.

"Could it be someone from one of your open cases?"

"Possibly, but I'm not close to naming a suspect in either the homicide or burglary."

"I'd say someone disagrees with you, Ruby. Someone thinks you're a threat."

"Can I ask what you're going to do about this?"

Grant picked up the letter and refolded it. "I haven't decided. I can't ignore it, but I don't want to play into the writer's hand and unfairly jeopardize your reputation. Right now, I'm leaning toward a quiet independent review of the allegation."

"All right."

"More importantly, I wanted to let you know someone's watching you. Be careful."

"I will."

Grant put the letter in his desk drawer and sat back in his chair. "Now, about the new fella who's joined your office."

"Jeremy Lawson."

"That's the one. What's your take?"

Ruby considered the question carefully before answering. The casual tone of Grant's question, meant to put her at ease, had the opposite effect. "I'll admit to being surprised when I found him at the office yesterday. I was aware of a discussion about giving the sheriff's office more reinforcements, but I hadn't realized a formal decision had been made." She folded her arms across her chest.

"There was no consultation among us either. It was all Tom."

Aha. Commissioner Tom Ewan. Again. Ruby hid her "I told you so" reaction to Grant's words. "I thought you folks always discussed every appointment."

Grant shrugged. "Usually, but not always. With the upcoming election, we've got full plates, so when Tom announced he'd arranged for a crime analyst to join the sheriff's office, we were happy to go along. Frankly, we've all been a little on edge, what with those serial burglaries. And even though it was after the fact, we took the discovery of the skeleton as a confirmation that Tom's idea to bring in an expert for consultation purposes was a good one."

"I see."

"Not that we don't have faith in you, but we've got to worry about public perception. Someone could start a rumor that Tinker is smack dab in the middle of an escalating crime wave and all we've done is sit on our hands."

"Well, one day's not much to go on." Ruby pursed her lips.

"Agreed, but I'm interested in your first impressions."

What were her first impressions? She closed her eyes for a moment and visualized Jeremy, always eager with his dark tousled hair, brown eyes, and swarthy complexion. He reminded her of a cute puppy, on the one hand seeking reassurance but, on the other, happy to destroy any shoe that crossed his path. In this case, order at the sheriff's office represented the shoe.

The incident at Rock Garden Park proved the point. Whether he meant to be or not, Jeremy was disruptive.

"He's a good man, but he seems prone to add chaos to our process," she said at last.

"Does he know what he's doing?"

"Tinker is unfamiliar territory. And he loves his

technology. If it were up to him, he'd outfit the office with every scientific gadget on the market. I'm not sure if it cramps his style when he's forced to use old-fashioned methods of investigation or if his mistakes stem from being unfamiliar with our practices. I understand he's been stuck behind a desk in New York for the past few years."

"Mistakes?"

Grant had zeroed in on the one word Ruby had hesitated to use. "How many mistakes can there be? He's only been in town a little over twenty-four hours."

"I shouldn't have called them mistakes. Let's just say I find his interruptions when I speak, and particularly while I'm interviewing a witness, annoying."

Grant grabbed a pencil to make a notation. "Lacks people skills," he read aloud.

"Not completely. He's established a rapport with Lucille Trefor." Ruby fixed Grant with an unblinking stare. "And everything he's done isn't all wrong. He's had some successes."

"Like?"

"He found three nails when we investigated a crime scene."

"Three, huh? Well then, this guy's definitely worth the money we're spending."

"Hey, it may not sound like much, but you never know what'll turn a case around—cigarette butts, paint flecks, three nails."

"Sorry. Inappropriate remark on my part."

"So, why the interest in Jeremy? What's really going on?"

Grant spent a full minute examining his fingernails. The pause gave Ruby a chance to think. At first her inclination to defend all coworkers had kicked in, and to be fair, one day didn't provide much of a window for her to form a judgment about Jeremy's value to the office.

But his arrival discombobulated her. Jeremy had already shown himself to be a meticulous investigator, respectful and eager to learn. All traits she admired. But in some respects he'd slowed her investigations. And his presence was a constant reminder that people had begun to question her ability to get the job done. No, instead of defending him, this might be an opportunity to get him sent back to New York.

Finally Grant looked at Ruby. "Off the record, Tom seems unusually excited about the appointment, which raises my suspicions. I wanted to get your take."

"Well, I won't cry if you decide to get him gone. I don't dislike Jeremy, but I work more efficiently without a gnat buzzing in my ear."

"Okay. I'll leave you to hammer out your working relationship." He pointed to the clock. "And that brings us to nine a.m., which is to say it's time for *Good Morning Tinker*. I never miss it."

Grant swiveled in his chair, turned a small television set to face him and Ruby, and pushed the On switch. Bess Trundle filled the screen. Then the camera panned back. She stood outside the municipal building, microphone in hand.

"They're right below us," Grant said. He turned up the volume.

"We're live here this morning with Commissioner Tom Ewan, who has exciting news about keeping Tinker safe. Take it away, Tom."

"Thanks, Bess. I'm delighted to introduce Jeremy Lawson to our esteemed viewers. He's our latest weapon in the war against crime."

A picture of Jeremy filled half the screen.

"This is exciting," Bess said. "Give us his credentials."

"Jeremy's a specialist, a crime analyst. His razor-sharp vision will cut through what I call the bad guy smoke and expose lawbreakers so they can be prosecuted to the fullest extent of the law."

"Sounds promising. Can you tell us more?"

"The people of Tinker have been terrorized by a burglar, who, frankly, seems to have gotten the best of our esteemed sheriff. I hope the addition of Jeremy changes the trajectory of this crime spree."

"You sound confident."

"I've always said, 'Keep Tinker safe,' and Jeremy Lawson is the fella to lead the charge. And when I'm reelected, I plan to convince the other commissioners to augment Jeremy's placement by increasing the allocation of funds for sheriff's services when our next budget is introduced. So remember the name, Jeremy Lawson. I hope my next report to the people will be to announce the apprehension of the burglar. Thank you."

Grant snorted and turned the television off. "Well, well, well. Trust Tom to make a bid for reelection and align himself with the crime-and-safety platform, all the while intimating the rest of us are against funding law enforcement endeavors. Plus, he all but pits you against Jeremy by lauding everything the people have gained with the addition of a crime analyst to the team."

"A crime analyst without the tools of his trade," Ruby added. "It's like asking someone to assemble a Rubik's Cube with only half the pieces."

"And even if this Jeremy fails, Tom can still say he tried. The man is a master manipulator."

"Well, I think the news report seals my fate, at least for the moment. I'm stuck with our esteemed crime analyst, so I best make the most of it."

Ruby waited inside the building until Tom had marched upstairs and the news crew had cleared off. With an effort, she put her thoughts about the poison pen letter on hold. All she could do was remain watchful and trust in God.

Odd that Tom had concentrated his speech and thereby directed public attention to the serial burglary instead of the discovery of the skeleton. Burglary was a property crime; the skeleton meant someone had died and, in this case, had been murdered. She knew all the commissioners were aware of the skeletal discovery, because Grant referenced it in their conversation. So, why downplay the homicide?

Maybe Tom figured a crime analyst had a better chance of solving a burglary than a murder. Or maybe, given the crime's age, a murderer on the loose no longer represented as big a threat to the public as an active prowler, in his opinion.

The irony of her predicament smacked into her full force. While most police personnel coped with a nonstop clamor to arrest culprits ASAP, she faced an almost universal disinterest in the murder. If the victim was Eleanor Costell, there were no relatives to apply pressure. Even the media, quick to react to anything crime-related, had mentioned but didn't pursue an angle of inquiry related to the discovery of the skeleton.

Did justice delayed mean justice forgotten? Not in Ruby Prescott's book.

When Ruby turned onto Pine Ridge Road a large campaign sign on the front lawn of Mayor Dosser's residence reminded her of the necessity of starting her own campaign. Although she'd been proclaimed sheriff at the last election, she still wondered why no one else had run for the office.

Was it because they refused to become associated with a law enforcement post where the previous person in charge had been tossed out for bad practices? Or had they acted out of pity and not opposed her candidacy in deference to her status as a widow?

Since taking office, she'd reestablished standards of fair treatment for everyone, which earned a compliment from Lucille, among others, although compliments could not guarantee another election victory. But she knew a case-closed stamp applied to both the murder and the serial burglary would trump a sign any day. Performance always spoke volumes over promises.

EIGHT

Jeremy eased his sports car into a parking space and hurried into the office. He heaved a sigh of relief, Ruby hadn't made it in yet, which meant he could grab a coffee, update his address book and transcribe his notes from yesterday's interview with the mayor.

Bottom line, the examination of the datebook all but proved that despite Lucille's allegations, Frank Dosser was not the burglar who'd overpowered Ruby at the theater. Checking his alibi was as simple as going on social media and seeing all the videos posted of his cousin's wedding in Fort Carson. The event had taken place Sunday evening, with the reception continuing until well after midnight. The only thing the esteemed mayor might be guilty of was staying up late.

Jeremy, who'd grown to like Frank when he'd interviewed him, was relieved he could be crossed off the suspect list. Eager to share his news, Jeremy half rose from his chair as Ruby entered the office. But Deborah buttonholed her, then called him over.

"You guys have to see this," she said. "It's a re-play of the *News at Nine*. Wait for it."

Jeremy could see Bess Trundle, who stood alongside Commissioner Tom Ewan while his own image overlooked the pair from its position at the top right corner of the screen. Jeremy widened his eyes.

Ruby stifled a groan. Forced to watch Commissioner Tom heap accolades on Jeremy while promoting his reelection platform wasn't any easier the second time through.

At the end of the news bit, Deborah closed her tablet.

"Really?" Jeremy looked at Deborah and Ruby. "What's the commissioner think he's doing?"

Ruby didn't hesitate. "I think he's assuming your work will overshadow everything we've been doing here for the past three-plus years and hopes the public will credit him with the idea of bringing you on board. It's all about votes."

"Cross your fingers that you don't have any undercover work coming down the pipe, 'cause your cover is blown. Not that we could keep your presence in Tinker a secret for long. It is a small town." Deborah winked.

Jeremy, who worried the others in the office might think he'd orchestrated or been in on the news briefing, chose his next words with care. "I'm embarrassed. My goal here is to fit in and work with people, not stand out as some sort of superhero. If you're correct and politics are behind the commissioner's behavior, I want no part of it."

Ruby shook her head. "No worries. Anyone can be bushwhacked. Now, if the excitement's passed, can we get back to work?"

As they assembled the incident room, Jeremy told Ruby his conclusions about Frank's whereabouts Sunday evening.

"I figured," Ruby said. "Much as I dislike him, I couldn't imagine it was Frank. Burglary requires stealth, and he leaves a trail like a slug. I do think Lucille was telling us the truth when she shared her observations about the culprit's distinctive walk though. It's something else we'll have to keep in mind."

An hour passed and Ruby rubbed her hands together. They'd listened to the recording of Lucille's statement again and studied photos of the crime scene. And when Jeremy wondered if the scarf and earring found in the trunk could be linked to Eleanor, Ruby agreed this required further investigation.

"Looks like we're done here. I've still got to hammer out next week's work schedules. In the meantime, Jeremy, why don't you give Lucille a call? The bones haven't been formally identified yet as Eleanor's, but we should still pursue every lead. It'd be useful to have a picture of our presumptive victim's life before she disappeared. As her best friend, Lucille might tell you something that will give us a direction."

He pulled out his phone and selected her number. After a minute, he pocketed the cell again. No answer. He'd have to try later.

Despite the ridiculous newscast, he noticed Ruby had changed her references from "my case" and "I" to "our case" and "us," which showed she was beginning to think of them as a team. Yep. Things were on the upswing. But he couldn't shake a niggling impression that something was bothering her. He'd caught her staring into space a lot today, her expression a cross between puzzlement and sadness. Did his presence still upset her?

When Jeremy entered the front office, Deborah raised her hands over her head and bowed from the waist. "All hail the superhero."

Jeremy rolled his eyes. "Please. I thought we put that to bed. I'll bet no one even sees the broadcast, much less believes it."

"Ya think?" Deborah raised the blind.

A group of twenty-some people, all seniors, had gathered in the parking lot. A few held signs with sayings like Our Hero and Save Our Town, which they pumped up and down as they chanted, "Jer-e-my," in unison. To make matters worse, Lucille led the crowd.

He blushed a deep red.

"You can't go out there," Ruby said, coming up behind them.

"She's right," Deborah agreed. "Step outside right now and they'll all want your autograph. You'd better stay inside and brace yourself. We may be mobbed." Her eyes twinkled.

Ruby chewed her lip, paused and then looked at Jeremy. "Would you be willing to front our float in the Thanksgiving parade? Maybe hang around after the event in a booth at the fair to shake hands and, yes, sign autographs?"

"You think that's really necessary?"

Ruby looked outside again. "I do."

"I can't believe you're serious. I think keeping a low profile until the hubbub dies down might be a better idea."

"We don't have that much time."

"Then I've got no choice," he agreed.

Ruby set her jaw and pushed open the door. The crowd surged forward. Deborah stayed in the doorway of the office and Jeremy peeked out the window. He wondered if Ruby would advance, which might force the group backward or stand her ground to act as a living barrier. She stood, feet hip width apart, rooted to the spot and folded her arms across her chest.

"Hello, folks. Welcome to the sheriff's office, I'm Ruby Prescott. Can I be of service?"

Lucille stepped forward and began talking to Ruby, who nodded and smiled. Ruby uncrossed her arms and adopted a more relaxed stance.

"What's going on?" Jeremy asked Deborah.

"I'd say Ruby pitched her idea about you giving out autographs at the Thanksgiving fair, and in return she's securing Lucille's agreement to do another interview."

"Oh, right, she probably told Lucille I needed to speak with her, but if I do it now, it could incite a riot."

"True."

"Does Ruby do this often?"

"What, broker a deal? All the time. It's one reason people no longer shudder when they have to deal with us. In my experience, people appreciate living in a town with law and order, so long as it's applied with a reasoned hand. What they won't tolerate is one law for them and one for 'friends of the sheriff's office.' So, how does it feel knowing you're being used as a bargaining chip?"

"Weird, but I'll take it."

"Okay, deal's done," Ruby said as she came back inside and slipped off her hat and jacket. "Just call Lucille in five and ask your questions. She's expecting to hear from you."

"Great. And what have I been committed to at the Thanksgiving festivities?"

"What I said before I went out there, with one addition."

"Oh?"

"I promised everyone if they left us today, anybody who attends the booth at the fair would get a handshake and an autographed headshot of you.

I'm visualizing an airbrushed image, sculpted face with a prominent curl on your forehead and a smile not unlike, well, a certain superhero. And a cape. Don't worry, there's a photographer in town." Ruby and Deborah dissolved in giggles.

Jeremy sighed. There was nothing left to do but phone Lucille on her cell.

"Let us pray."

Pastor Emeritus Henry Miller, who insisted he be called Pastor Hank, had cheeks which reminded Jeremy of a road map with a network of wrinkles instead of streets. Pastor Hank settled Ruby and Jeremy on the porch in chairs arranged in a semicircle to allow for a view of his special garden, populated with only native flora and which stretched for one hundred feet in front of a stand of aspens.

"Nice spread. I hope our conversation doesn't take too much time away from your fall cleanup schedule," Ruby said.

The pastor's blue eyes gleamed. "Don't worry. The maxim for this type of garden is to go slow, makes it easier for someone in their nineties, like me. Everything here attracts pollinators and encourages natural processes. I guess all natural has become the way of the world. They keep telling me it's all about balance. Words I try to live by."

Amen. Jeremy studied the raw beauty of the space and wondered if this might be him one day.

As much as he liked the hustle and bustle of a city, there was something about Tinker and its landscape that was starting to win him over.

Pastor Hank reached for a pair of pruning shears and snipped the air. "I don't deadhead often. I prefer to let them go to seed. It will ultimately give me more plants anyway. The dried stalks, I call them stick guardians, are left standing even after a frost to ensure any stray insect eggs and seeds they may shelter are available to the wintering birds."

"Interesting." Jeremy had never heard of a garden of only native plants.

Pastor Hank set down the shears, rubbed his hands together. "You say Lucille Trefor gave you my name? I trust she's well but can't say I've seen her often in the past several years. And you're here to talk to me about the skeleton you found?"

Ruby nodded. "It's been identified as Eleanor Costell."

"You're sure?"

"Yes. Dental records provided the final confirmation."

"Horrible. Of course I remember Eleanor. She was a member of my Bible study group. Everybody thought she'd moved to Hollywood to try her luck as an actor, and all the while she lay in the theater. Do you think a stranger is responsible?"

Ruby ducked her head a moment before speaking. "I'm sorry, Pastor, no. I'm pretty sure Eleanor knew her killer. Several facts about the crime, including the location of the bones, suggest this was not the work of a stranger."

"Oh." Pastor Hank bowed his head. "The breach of trust involved in being killed by someone you know makes it uglier, if that's possible."

Ruby's voice quavered. "It's my first murder. You see pictures of crime scenes in the academy, but it's not the same. I wonder sometimes how one human being could do that to another."

Jeremy saw her shiver. It wasn't a reaction to the cold, more as if she needed to shake herself free from a shroud of self-doubt.

"Although you folks bear bad news, I'm happy to help in any way I can." The pastor gazed into the distance. He pointed to a white-breasted bird perched on an aspen branch. "Eleanor's personality was not unlike the nuthatch you see before you, active and agile with lots of initiative."

"You never doubted she'd left for Hollywood?" Ruby asked.

"Not really. She didn't present as unhappy, you understand, but she liked to push the boundaries, as they say today. If you'll pardon the cliché, the phrase 'the grass is always greener' would be an apt summation of her perspective."

Ruby tapped her finger on her cheek and seemed to be waiting for the pastor to continue.

"You know, we can learn a lot from birds. Take your nuthatch here. It will forage on its own, but it becomes braver when joined by chickadees. Eleanor too enjoyed and often relied on the support of others. So while her leaving didn't surprise me, the fact she left by herself did take me aback."

Ruby had pulled out a small notepad and pen. "Tell me about the other members of the Bible study group."

Pastor Hank rubbed his knees.

"Let me see. The group consisted of five people—Eleanor Costell, Lucille Trefor, Billy Jenkins, Anna Jones and Harvey Klingshot. We were in our second year when Eleanor left. Lucille had a difficult time after that, and the group disbanded within the month."

"Can you talk about the group dynamics?"

"Certainly. Eleanor always asked interesting questions that sparked discussions, sometimes heated. Lucille was a little less outspoken, but she definitely encouraged Eleanor. Harvey Klingshot fancied himself a ladies' man—I think that's the phrase that was used back then. He may have been going out with Eleanor. Billy and Anna were sweet on each other."

The pastor smiled at the recollection. "Do they still say 'sweet on' today?"

"Lucille does," Jeremy said.

Ruby grinned at him, and Jeremy's heart skipped beat. Before he could figure that one out, she'd turned back to Pastor Hank.

"How heated were the discussions?" Ruby asked.

"Oh, it's just my manner of speaking. No one raised their voice in anger. I encouraged debate, not fisticuffs."

"Do you remember any animosity among the members?"

"Perhaps a little rivalry between Harvey and Billy. Harvey would pay Eleanor extra attention and pull out a chair for her, that sort of thing. After this had gone on awhile, I noticed some friction between the two boys. But I know Billy had no romantic interest in Eleanor, and in conjunction with his reputation, Harvey flirted freely."

"Four of the five in your group also involved themselves in the theater. Were the four actors cliquish?"

"No, to the contrary, they were walking advertisements for our mission statement, 'All are welcome.'"

"Lucille didn't get pulled into any romantic entanglements?"

"Oh, she had a steady boyfriend, someone outside the study group, though I can't remember his name offhand."

"How did Anna relate to the other girls?" Jeremy asked.

"The word 'cordial' springs to my lips, but they were closer. Friends. When coming into the room, I'd often find the three of them with their heads together, giggling." Pastor Hank smiled. "Anna was the smartest. She had an innate ability to see nuances in the Scriptures. Eleanor was the shining light and Lucille was her sidekick."

"And they seemed happy with their roles?" Ruby paused.

Pastor Hank scratched his head. "Overall, yes. I'd say at times Lucille held herself back to accommodate Eleanor. And Anna was slightly more independent and less susceptible to the influence of others. She walked her own path. But they were a happy, inquisitive group and a pleasure to teach."

"One more thing," Ruby said. "Did any of the girls have accessories they favored?"

"Eleanor enjoyed jewelry, but then they all liked to look nice."

Ruby snapped her notebook closed, but Jeremy cupped his chin in his hand. "I'm curious," he said. "You look settled here with the garden and such, but I imagine you used to be very active. Has the transition to retirement been difficult compared to what had been your daily routine for fifty-odd years?"

"Initially I worried. I thought I'd miss my role as senior pastor, but I was wrong. I loved my work, but I've got more on the go now than ever. The garden takes a lot of my time. And I always indulge in a daily nap after lunch. But the big story is I'm starting a newsletter."

Jeremy leaned forward. "A newsletter? That is exciting. Tell me about it."

NINE

While the men discussed Pastor Hank's latest project, Ruby remembered her own years of Bible study. Scripture had provided the foundation for her hopes and dreams, plans that included a tour of duty in the military, which strengthened her sense of purpose and commitment to God. No regrets.

Upon discharge, her training and certification as a police officer was a natural choice. She welcomed romance and marriage. Life was full. She met every challenge, eyes open, arms wide. She smiled at the memories. And when tragedy struck, it was her bedrock belief and trust in God that had sustained her.

Hearing her name shook Ruby out of her reverie and she looked at the duo.

It seemed Pastor Hank's response to Jeremy mimicked the way Lucille had reacted when she'd been asked to elaborate on her bird-watching activities. The pastor sat up straighter, and his color improved as he described the plans for an online newsletter.

As she listened, Henry's enthusiasm captured her interest, until Jeremy took the opportunity to be quintessentially Jeremy.

She smothered a grin as Jeremy explained to Henry why he should feature a double opt-in for newsletter subscribers.

"It's protection against hackers, someone mischievous or someone with a grudge."

"But I'm in no danger," Pastor Hank insisted.

"Still the double opt-in is simple. Instead of just accepting anyone who clicks Subscribe to your newsletter, new subscribers are sent a separate email asking them to click and confirm their subscription. If the initial subscribers are bogus entities with emails obtained from the dark net, there won't be a second click. Your email will be ignored and your subscriber list will be safe. With a double opt-in you've got everything to gain and nothing to lose."

"Is it easy to set up?"

"Come on. We'll do it together."

"Together" took a while.

Fair enough. Pastor Hank did seem delighted with Jeremy's help and suggestions, and she'd had the time to handle a couple of calls from Deborah.

"If we hurry we can snag a couple of plates at the infamous Daily Buffet." Ruby opened the car door.

"Sorry it took so long. I get embroiled."

As they drove to the restaurant, Ruby considered asking Jeremy about his obsession with new technology. But she had to admit it did help him establish a bond with people. Plus, the habit increased the camaraderie between the sheriff's office and the population of Tinker. Why then did she find his ways so irritating at times?

Ruby decided to put a hold on the topic, at least until after lunch. If she stepped into muddy waters, it would be on a full stomach.

"Delicious," Jeremy said. "Another place to put on my favorites list. So now that we've got a minute, how'd you rate my first two days at the job?"

Ruby put down her fork and chose her words carefully. "Overall, you've been helpful. But I find your advice about the benefits of adding gadgets and programs to our arsenal a little annoying."

"I get that. I'll try to put on the brakes." He finished off his coffee. "But in my defense, I've spent the last few years surrounded by sophisticated software programs, programs that can spit out an answer to a question in less than half the time it would take a person to figure things out on their own. Technological knowledge simplifies and sheds light on sticky problems."

"And it brought you here."

Jeremy lowered his chin to his chest and cast his eyes downward but said nothing.

Ruby reached across the table and touched Jeremy's arm. "I'm sorry. I didn't mean to imply being here is a step backward for you."

"I didn't think you meant it that way. I'm glad to be here."

"Are you finding the learning curve steep?"

"A bit."

"Then I should lighten up." Ruby looked Jeremy in the eyes. "You realize this is the first time we've been able to relax."

"True. It's been go go go since I arrived." Jeremy smiled.

"Actually, I like to know who I'm working with."

"Me too, and I'm happy to answer all your questions."

"Great. Married or single?"

Wow. There were a million questions she could have started with, everything from the old "What's your favorite color?" to the mundane "What's your favorite sport?" to the more esoteric "Why do you think we dream?" But, no, she'd blurted out the one intrusive question which might make Jeremy think she had a romantic interest in him.

"Single. You?"

"Widowed. Four years ago."

"I'm sorry."

"Thanks." Ruby tried to adopt a nonchalant tone. "It's taken a while for me to think of myself as single." She covered the awkward moment by asking another question. "Any family back in New York?"

"A sister, two years my junior. She's got a husband and a son."

He dug into his pocket, extracted a wallet, and pulled out a snapshot with dog-eared corners.

"I'd take my nephew, David, to Coney Island for a day trip every chance I got in the summer. There are lots of shots of us on my phone, but I carry this one with me."

When he placed it on the table, Ruby could see Jeremy standing with his arm around a young boy of about seven, against the backdrop of an amusement park that featured a huge Ferris wheel.

Ruby pointed at the ride. "You'd never get me up there. I'm kinda uncomfortable with heights."

"Wonder Wheel gives people an incredible view of Deno's amusement park. After dark, red and yellow lights line the circumference and spokes. It's quite the landmark."

"I can imagine."

"David and I loved it. Same routine each trip—a spin around the world when we got to the park and one before we left. It bookmarked our day, which always included a ride or five on the Cyclone coaster and dogs for lunch at Nathan's."

"Sounds wonderful."

"When I look at the picture, I smell fried food and hear barkers hawking carnival games. In my mind's eye I see crowds of people and feel the sun on my skin. Those were good times. Is there an amusement park in these parts?"

"We've got a penny arcade downtown and a Santa's Workshop at the North Pole in Colorado Springs. I'll bet your nephew would love playing pinball or seeing a magic show. And I'm pretty sure Santa's Workshop has rides. I've always wanted to check it out but so far haven't gotten around to it."

"Not even when you were a kid?"

"Not even. My parents were naturalists. They loved to hike and spent all their spare time outdoors. My dad and I would track and photograph birds and animals. Lots of fun, but I used to be jealous of classmates who told tales of carnival games and rides at the amusement park. On the upside, I know these woods like a pancake knows syrup."

"Knowledge that makes you uniquely qualified for the job."

"I guess. It's not something I've thought about a lot."

"You know a bit about my background. What about you? Have you always lived in New York?"

"Yes, ma'am. New Yorker born and raised. I was a crime buff who loved statistics, so I attended college in Boston, got my first job back in New York and began to climb the career ladder."

"I've always thought of New York City as a pressure cooker."

"It can be. I juggled a lot of heavy expectations at my work and got used to most of it. At first, I relied on my faith to sustain me, but as I climbed higher, I began to drift from God, something I've begun to regret."

"Do you have any relations in these parts?"

"No."

"Then you'll miss your sister and nephew even more."

"I will, but there are always video calls."

"That's not the same."

"No, it's not."

"I think that's your first admission that technology isn't the solution to everything." Ruby sat back in her seat and rubbed her hands together. "So, I'm looking at a frontier man, heading west from the Big Apple into the great unknown. Something compelling must have convinced you to leave New York."

Jeremy paused, then shifted in his seat. A slight frown darkened his features for a split second.

The long silence weighed on Ruby and she tugged on her shirt.

"It was time for a change," he said at last.

Jeremy's transfer to Tinker obviously touched a nerve. Ruby didn't think an apology appropriate but vowed to avoid the subject in the future.

"What do people do in Tinker after dark?" Jeremy's chipper demeanor had returned.

"Not a heck of a lot. I think it goes back to our

roots as a town. Tinker encourages artists and naturalists to set up shop, people who tend to go to bed early and rise with the sun. There are a couple of restaurants that remain open a bit later, more to cater to the summer tourists than locals, and even the community theater restricts its run to weekend matinees."

"Should I get used to early bedtimes?"

"That or take up reading. Oh, and there are churches."

"At night?"

"Yes, with plenty of activities going on in the evening. You mentioned moving away from God. Do you go to church?"

"Sunday school was a part of my routine as a kid, not so much lately."

"Well, you're welcome to join me anytime. I attend services every Sunday morning, unless there's a work emergency, of course."

Ruby almost cringed. She'd started this conversation with a question about Jeremy's marital status and seemed to be ending it with a suggestion they attend church together. Would he think she was angling for a date?

"Church would be nice. I've been thinking for a while now… I should be dedicating myself more to it. My spiritual life is important to me."

"Great. Now, I suggest we try to catch at least one of the people Pastor Hank pointed us toward. It's just coming up on two o'clock, and most of the

older population can be found at our senior rec-
reation center weekday afternoons, so we may as
well head over there now."

Jeremy kept his head down as they walked to
the car. He hadn't expected to exchange so much
personal information with Ruby over lunch. He
rarely talked about himself but had to admit his
opening up had encouraged Ruby to share more
about herself.

As they reached the car, he could see a piece
of paper under the windshield wiper and had to
stop himself from reaching out to grab it. A chill
ran down his neck. Words, written with a black
marker, spelled out a warning. *I'm Watching You.*

Ruby picked the paper up by a corner and
bagged it. "I doubt we'll get fingerprints, but we
have to try."

"The burglar?" he asked.

"Not likely. I've been on that case for six
months and no one's so much as blinked. More
likely the murderer. They must think we're getting close."

Jeremy shook his head. "But we're not."

"I'd say someone disagrees with you. If only
we knew who."

Although Ruby kept her voice neutral, Jeremy
noticed her movements had become more abrupt.
This warning's creeped me out too.

Ruby started the car and turned left, but Jeremy noticed she kept glancing in her rear view mirror. "What?"

"I'm not sure."

Jeremy could hear the hesitation in her voice.

"I feel like we're being followed but there's not another car on the road."

Overactive imagination? Maybe, though Jeremy couldn't shake the feeling someone was observing them, either. "I'd suggest we take evasive action, but the street's empty."

"True," Ruby agreed.

Jeremy pulled out his smartphone and aimed it around the car's interior while Ruby continued to drive. "If there's a hidden camera anywhere in here, it'll show as a red dot," he said.

"How would someone get it into our car?"

"They wouldn't and didn't, I guess." Jeremy put the phone back in his pocket. "Still, we'd be well advised to keep our eyes open."

"Always do," Ruby said.

The Tinker Senior Center sat on the east side of Pine Ridge Road. Cars filled the parking lot. A cluster of people watched the last match of the lawn bowling season that pitted the Tinker Mavericks against the Colorado Springs Bears.

Ruby had told him the building, with its large windows and refurbished exterior, had been converted from an old rug company, a project townspeople considered a wise investment of tax dollars.

A bell tinkled when they arrived, a reminder for them to check in at the reception area stationed to their left.

A woman who looked to be in her midforties wore her shoulder-length hair behind her ears, a style which added width to her face. But she didn't just sit at the reception counter, she commandeered her cubbyhole office like the admiral of a ship, and from her demeanor, Jeremy guessed every object she'd require for the job had been arranged within striking distance of her swivel chair.

She looked up as he and Ruby approached and said, "Howdy, partners."

"Hey, Janice. Let me introduce the newest member of my team. Jeremy, this is Janice Cap, receptionist extraordinaire and the heart of the center. What she doesn't know probably isn't worth knowing. Janice, say hello to Jeremy Lawson."

"Hi." Janice grinned and addressed Ruby. "Am I dreaming? I'm sure I saw this strong fella featured on the morning news show, and I'd say he looks even cuter in the flesh. All kidding aside, Jeremy, it's nice to meet you. To what do I owe this visit?"

Ruby ignored her irritation at Janice kidding Jeremy and pulled a list out of her pocket. "I'm hoping to catch up with either Harvey Klingshot or Anna Jones. Have you seen them today?"

Janice answered without hesitation. "You probably missed Harvey. He's a fixture weekday mornings. Within fifteen minutes of our opening, he arms himself with coffee, parks in the lounge and holds court with the same group of four other men who trickle in over the next thirty minutes. I call them the Gang of Five. The newspaper fuels their discussions, which can get lively."

"A mornings-only man."

"Correct. Once, several years ago, he registered for an afternoon arts class because he'd seen one on TV. Fancied himself a real Michelangelo, but he only lasted one session."

"Not his thing, huh?"

"I guess. Now Anna Jones is a different story. She's aloof. Sticks to herself and haunts the library."

A loud crash stopped Janice.

Jeremy could hear shouts coming from the rear of the building.

Janice frowned. "Not good. Sounds like Julia Holmes is off her meds. Third time this month." She started to rise from her chair, but Ruby motioned for her to resume her seat.

"You stay here. If it's a medication issue, I can intervene unofficially." Ruby turned and jogged down the hall.

Jeremy followed.

TEN

Jeremy could see two toppled chairs from his place at the doorway. He guessed the large up-ended tray was the source of the crashing noise he'd heard earlier. Bingo supplies, including cards, plastic containers and chips, lay scattered on the floor. His foot skidded as he tried to step forward. Several of the brightly colored plastic disks caught under the sole of his shoe. But he didn't feel embarrassed as he lost and then recovered his balance. Nobody noticed him. All eyes were on the women in the aisle that separated the tables.

A tall skinny lady with braided gray hair and steel-rimmed glasses appeared to be trying to moderate a dispute. Jeremy thought the two combatants could be sisters, with their white hair permed into tight curls, perfect circles of red rouge on full cheeks and round lips.

Their faces contorted with anger. Both held fast to each end of a red-and-green plaid towel. As they pulled and tried to wrench the cloth out of the other person's hands, Jeremy worried the tug of war would end with one or both opponents splayed on the floor.

"You're cheating," the short, stout woman on the left shouted.

"No, I'm not. You're a liar." The other woman, slightly taller and heavier, huffed out a series of grunts and continued to pull.

"Are so."

"Am not."

The first woman, aggrieved about the supposed cheating, tugged the towel again but added a downward motion combined with a twist. The second, in the process of leaning backward, lost her footing, slipped and landed in an undignified heap on the floor.

Everyone surged forward as Ruby extended her hands and pulled the fallen woman to her feet.

"My name is Sheriff Ruby Prescott. Give us room, please, everyone. Step back and let me get her to a seat." Ruby escorted the woman over to a chair and eased her into it.

A murmur ran through the crowd.

Wow. That was easy. Jeremy admired Ruby, whose laser-sharp decisiveness continued to surprise him. But no sooner had Ruby straightened when the miscreant, armed with plaid towel, flicked the end toward her rival, who was still catching her breath.

"Everyone settle down. That includes you, ma'am, with the towel. Stop and sit over there."

Ruby pointed to a vacant chair. "Now, what's going on?"

"She cheated."

"Did not."

The accuser wagged her finger at the woman she accused of foul play. "You called Bingo when you saw me getting close. You knew you didn't have one, but you called Bingo anyway. You figured I'd take my chips off my cards to get ready for the next game while you called out your numbers. And that's what happened. So when the game resumed, it was too late. I'd cleared my cards. Your antics halved the field by the time the round continued. It's not fair."

"I made a mistake, is all."

"A mistake you seem to make at least once a week," one of the other women chimed in. "Judy's right. Miranda does cheat."

The volume of voices reached greater heights as everyone weighed in on the renewed accusation.

"If you're such a hotshot, Sheriff, arrest her," Miranda shouted. "She's falsely accused me. That's a crime. Then there's the matter of the assault."

"What assault? *You* attacked *me*, and when I defended myself, you fell backward."

"I didn't attack you. You're exaggerating and that's another crime. You just keep racking them up." Miranda pointed her finger at Judy.

"Huh."

"Huh yourself. All I did was try to rescue my

lucky towel, which you stole. You're guilty of false accusations, assault, theft and maybe inciting a riot. If this sheriff knows anything about her job, it's the big house for you." Beads of perspiration lined Miranda's forehead.

"Now who's guilty of exaggeration?" Judy folded her arms over her chest.

"And what about my towel? You have to give it back." Miranda glared at her main accuser and stuck out her hand.

"I'll do nothing of the sort." Judy stuffed the lucky towel under her bottom.

Check and checkmate? Jeremy refrained from smiling.

Miranda appealed to Ruby. "Did you see what she just did?"

Ruby turned to Judy. "Come on. Give it here."

Judy reluctantly handed the towel over to Ruby, who handed it to Miranda.

"Well, what about it, Sheriff? It's time to haul Judy off to jail." Miranda stuck out her chin, a defiant gesture which succeeded in working the crowd into a new frenzy.

Jeremy could hear snatches of conversation.

"Miranda cheats."

"Not true. Her forgetfulness is legendary."

"She's a bad one, for sure."

"I like Miranda. She lent me her reading glasses when mine broke."

"She's a drama queen."

"What about Judy? We all know she's a bully."

Jeremy saw Ruby shut her eyes and pinch the bridge of her nose. He could imagine her frustration. This was nothing more than a Bingo game. How high could the stakes be? What would it take to bring these seniors to their senses? And suddenly he knew what to do.

Without warning, he started to walk through the crowd toward the center of the group. At first, everyone continued their chatter. But after he'd taken enough steps to make sure most eyes were on him, he stopped and gazed at the assembled group. "Friends—"

"Hey, who is that?" Judy asked. "Is that Bob's son, come from Denver?"

The group shushed Judy and Jeremy had the floor again.

"Friends, there are times when all of us have to remember that we need to treat others as we'd like to be treated. You folks probably have known and lived next to each other a long time, you have to extend a little common courtesy now and again, and that means solving problems with calm heads and voices."

The woman with the braid who'd tried to mediate the dispute earlier was nodding vigorously.

Jeremy smiled. "As I'm sure you've all heard, the sheriff has a lot on her plate, and you don't want to add to her concerns, now do you?"

The lady with the braid had switched to shaking her head. A number of the others looked contrite, especially Judy and Miranda.

Jeremy could see Ruby trying to hide a smile, so he bent down and righted the overturned chairs.

A white-haired lady smiled sheepishly and spoke up, "It's just a misunderstanding between friends. Sometimes these things crop up, though they usually don't require police intervention."

"We happened to be here on other business," Ruby said. "Glad to be of help."

"If you ladies aren't more careful, the center will stop offering Bingo. These outbursts ruin the game and disrupt an otherwise pleasant afternoon," the woman wearing the braid said sternly. She began to move empty chairs back to their places. Others picked up the supplies scattered on the floor. Soon everyone, even Miranda and Judy, had resumed their seats.

As the woman with the braid, who also turned out to be the Bingo caller, moved to the front and spoke into the microphone, Ruby and Jeremy left room.

"That was a touch of genius," Ruby said.

"It was nothing." Jeremy shrugged. "First rule of police work I learned was how to de-escalate a tense situation. Always stuck with me."

"Well, it certainly worked this time." Ruby let out a sigh. "Policing disputes at the Senior Center, who knew? Let's hope our interview with Anna Jones doesn't involve as much excitement."

* * *

When Jeremy and Ruby walked into the library at the center, they entered a different world. Silence reigned supreme. Windows spanned the length of the long wall of the rectangular room and allowed for an abundance of light. The outside activity created an ever-changing backdrop. Bookshelves lined the other three walls and two Queen Anne wing-backed chairs were arranged in front of a decorative fireplace.

"Only thing missing is a cat," Jeremy murmured.

"The cat was rehomed two months ago. Allergies," Ruby replied.

A slight woman sat at a reading table in a simple wooden chair positioned so her back faced the windows. Her short straight hair, lack of jewelry and rigid posture spoke to a stoic nature.

Jeremy walked over to her. "You must be Anna Jones."

The woman turned her book down on the table and looked up. "I am. And you are?"

After introducing themselves, Jeremy paused while he formulated his next question, but Anna spoke up immediately.

"Why would the sheriff or her deputy be interested in me?"

Jeremy was about to clarify his role at the station but chose instead to say, "We're investigating the death of Eleanor Costell. I believe you used to know her."

"I listen to the news and read the paper. You mean 'murder,' don't you?" Her voice rose. "You're investigating Eleanor's murder. Death indeed. There's no need to sugarcoat your words, young man. Say what you mean."

Chastised, Jeremy reached into his pocket. He placed a photograph on the table. "I'd like you to look at this, please."

The snapshot showed Lucille, Eleanor and Anna, all three teenagers smiling for the camera.

Anna touched her finger to it. "I suppose you expect me to say something quaint, such as 'those were the days' or 'we looked so young,' but I see three girls leaning against a fence rail during a break in rehearsal. Three bored girls under all those cheerful faces. I remember thinking later, 'No wonder Eleanor decided to take off.'"

"Except now we know she didn't," Jeremy said.

"Yes." She gazed away, presumably caught up in the life and times of over fifty years ago.

Jeremy interrupted her thoughts. "Eleanor's disappearance didn't strike you as odd?"

"No. At the time, I envied her and afterward I used to wonder what would've happened if I'd left Tinker with Billy. He asked me, you know, to explore, experience something other than small-town life. But I was afraid to go and he refused to leave without me."

"I sense guilt," Ruby said.

"I've always asked myself, would things have worked out differently for him? You know he died within a few months of Eleanor's disappearance?"

"We were told," Jeremy said.

"So here we are. You've shown me this picture and forced me to relive a painful time. How does that help your investigation?"

"We're interested in Eleanor's relationships."

"Relationships? I knew it. You're trying to develop what they now call 'persons of interest,' and you suspect me."

Ruby softened her voice. "'Suspect' is a strong word. But to solve a homicide, you've got to learn about the victim, so we're speaking to her associates. Do you mind if we sit down?"

"Please do. So, I'm not a suspect, I'm an associate. All right, I may not believe you, but I'll play along. I would say Eleanor and I tolerated each other. We competed for grades and acting roles and, until Billy came along, boys."

"When we spoke to Pastor Hank, he described you girls as friends who often had your heads together giggling."

"Well, appearances can be deceiving. In the context of a Bible study group, we'd hardly want to convey the impression to the pastor of any animosity. After all, the Bible says to love one another. Others in the group, like Harvey or Lucille, would be able to give you a more accurate assessment of how everyone got along."

"But what's your assessment?" Ruby raised her eyebrows.

"Eleanor had the biggest personality. She was the tallest and, in my opinion, the cutest. I'll admit I often felt outclassed. Sometimes we'd argue. Once the argument turned physical. She pulled my hair and I may have shoved her away. Told her off good. But I didn't kill her."

Jeremy continued the questioning. "Did you go to the theater the day Eleanor disappeared?"

"Let me think." Anna furrowed her brow and remained silent for a minute. "I doubt it," she said at last. "My recollection is that it was a day like any other. I'd have figured Eleanor and Lucille would be at the theater running lines, and I wanted to be alone with Billy. After school he and I may have stayed at my place and practiced our lines or gone downtown for a soda."

Jeremy flipped back through his notepad. "Someone else recollects Billy, upset by the news his mom and yours were fighting, went to the theater to tell Lucille he couldn't be in the play any longer."

"Someone? You mean Lucille. How convenient. The two people who could corroborate that story, Eleanor and Billy, are dead. If Billy was being pressured to quit the play, he'd have told me, and he didn't. He'd never have gone to the theater and spoken to Lucille first."

"Not even because she, or rather her family, owned the theater and were producing the play?"

"Not even."

"Okay." Jeremy pointed to the picture again. "Do you remember the play you were rehearsing?"

"*Costume Party*. The opening date was three weeks away when the picture you showed me was taken, but after Eleanor left, our enthusiasm for the project died. Sorry, poor choice of words."

"Lucille's necklace is beautiful. A prop, I assume?"

Anna picked up the snapshot for a closer look. "I don't think so. Lucille always decked herself out like royalty, a reminder to everyone that she came from money. I'm sure the props in the play couldn't come close to matching the look or price of this little bauble."

"You described Eleanor as outclassing you. Did it bother you that Lucille had more spending money?"

"That question makes me sound small, but no, it didn't. You have to understand, Eleanor was the real deal, as they say, so I felt jealous. But Lucille only had money, and money by itself doesn't take a person very far."

Jeremy pocketed the picture. "Tell us about another member of the theater group, Harvey Klingshot."

"Harvey was Eleanor's boyfriend. He probably took this picture."

"Was he a popular fellow?"

"Among us? More or less, though he'd sometimes go through the motions, say one thing, but do another. He'd express undying love for Eleanor, all the while seeing other girls behind her back. He thought himself irresistible, at least to anyone in a dress." Anna's nose twitched.

"You really didn't like the actors in the theater group, did you?"

"Admittedly, I wasn't close to them, but that doesn't make me a murderer."

"I agree." Jeremy smiled. "Is there any significance to the fact you five belonged to both the Bible study and theater groups?"

"No significance at all. Tinker's small. Paths of people intersect, though I guess coming from New York, you wouldn't be familiar with that phenomenon."

Jeremy suppressed a groan. He wondered if everyone here knew his background. "Did you enjoy the Bible study group?"

"Yes. I'd accepted God into my life as a young girl and wanted to learn more. The group met once a week to read a section of Scripture and discuss its meaning."

"Did you notice any friction among the participants?"

"No. Eleanor enjoyed tossing ideas back and

forth, so she challenged the pastor, always questioning. We observed, watched the drama unfold and soaked up information by osmosis. I learned a lot about my place in God's world. And speaking of the world, I've written my name and address on this slip of paper in case you need to speak to me again."

"Thanks." Ruby pocketed the information before asking her final question. "Do you have any idea who might have killed Eleanor?"

"None at all. She and I weren't close enough to share secrets. I've admitted we were rivals, but I didn't harm her and can't imagine any of the rest of the gang hurting her either. Billy and I were involved with each other. Eleanor and Lucille were best friends. Eleanor and Harvey dated. Besides, who in a Bible study group would break the sixth commandment, 'Thou shalt not kill'?"

ELEVEN

They caught up to Harvey Klingshot backstage at the Second Grand Theater, which was sandwiched between a camera store and a souvenir shop on Main Street.

Ruby sized him up: tall, at six foot one, with blue eyes and a head of thick dark hair that would make many his age, which she estimated to be early eighties, jealous. A birthmark the shape of a bird on his neck was a surprise.

"You're here for the audition," he said as he pumped Ruby's hand with enough vigor to drive her through the floor. "You're in the wrong place, but before you go, I've got just the thing."

He disappeared into a dressing room and reappeared with two autographed headshots. "I give these to everyone. One day a show, a movie, TV episode you're in may just need an actor, and when it does, think of me. My contact number's on the back." He smiled then threw his shoulders back, extended his arms and broke into a song.

"Thanks," Ruby said after he'd finished.

"I didn't realize the next play featured a law person, but the cowboy hat and handcuffs on your belt add an authentic touch, and we both know it's all about the look."

"It's more than a look," Ruby said. "I am the sheriff."

Harvey smacked his hand against his forehead. "Of course you are. Ruby Prescott. So you've decided to try acting. Great choice. It'll be a feather in our cap to list you as a cast member."

"No. I'm not here for an audition. We—this is Jeremy Lawson, by the way—came by in the hopes of speaking to you."

"Well then, this is your lucky day. Here I am, at your service." Harvey bowed.

Ruby smiled. "Is there somewhere we could talk? It's crowded in the hall."

"Sure. We can use the greenroom, and I'll get us some coffee while we're at it."

Harvey directed them to a room painted a pale blue, situated downstairs beneath the stage. A cluster of upholstered chairs and sofas were grouped around a coffee table littered with sheets of paper. Jeremy sat at one end of a two-seater sofa in the hopes that Ruby would sit beside him, but she selected a chair on the diagonal.

Harvey frowned as he cleared a space on the table for three cups. "Kids, they refuse to take responsibility for their scripts. Scripts are the lifeline of actors. Leaving them lying around, no excuse for it." He settled beside Jeremy. "Now, how can I help you?"

Ruby sipped her coffee then asked, "Do you remember Eleanor Costell?"

"Of course I remember her. Lovely gal. When I heard she'd been found at the old theater, I about flipped my lid. We'd dated some. Folks back then said she'd taken off for Hollywood. I didn't believe it at first. She hadn't warned me she was leaving town, and I expected if she were serious she'd invite me to go along, not that I would have said yes."

"You're the first person we've talked to who didn't automatically accept that she'd left." Ruby put her coffee mug on the table. "Did you follow it up, express doubt about the story to the sheriff at the time?"

"No. What would I say? That I couldn't believe a girl I dated wouldn't invite me along for what might be the biggest adventure of her life? I recall being miffed though. She could have slipped me a hint she was really going to go. I mean this was Hollywood, after all, but it makes sense now. In retrospect, she left Tinker, just not the way she'd planned." He cleared his throat. "I guess that makes me sound callous."

"Well…" Ruby's voice trailed away.

"Do you remember any problems she was having with people?" Jeremy asked.

"I hate to gossip, but Eleanor and Anna argued

all the time. They competed in school for marks and for friends. Oil and water as the saying goes. But the big surprise for me was that she hung with Lucille so much."

"Why?" Ruby's radar tingled. No one else had suggested trouble lurked between the two best friends.

"Their relationship struck me a bit odd." Harvey shrugged. "On the one hand, you had a rich girl with no discernible personality and, on the other, a girl with less money but bushels of character. As we say in the business, Eleanor had a presence to which Lucille could only aspire. Oh, they got along, were rarely seen apart, but Eleanor drove that relationship."

Ruby hesitated and considered Harvey's summary of the power dynamic between the two girls.

Harvey leaned forward, his brows raised. "You don't believe me? Look at Lucille's behavior. After Eleanor took off, Lucille acted like a rudderless boat. She couldn't force herself to enter the Grand Theater again. She dropped out of acting and abandoned career plans, at least according to rumors. She holed up in that house, the same house she lives in today, and just stopped. I'm no doctor, but these things add up to someone possibly wrestling with a big depression."

"Yet you'll confirm you weren't aware of any problems Eleanor had with Lucille before her disappearance?"

"Not a one. Even if she disagreed with Eleanor, I doubt Lucille would have spoken up, too afraid of jeopardizing the relationship."

Harvey took a deep breath. "I shouldn't say this, but if you're looking for problems, Eleanor's biggest one may have been me. Sometimes I went out with other girls, but I was careful to make sure she never found out. Juggling admirers was my younger self's biggest challenge." He winked at Ruby and nudged Jeremy with his elbow.

"What's your take on the others in the group, Anna Jones and Billy Jenkins?"

"Anna and Billy were okay, got along with everyone, but they only had eyes for each other."

"Did either of them talk about any problems with the production?"

"Not to my knowledge."

"Did they spend much time around the old theater doing things like practicing their parts?"

Harvey thought a moment. "No, they didn't. They practiced with each other. Anna had a large swing on the front porch and I'd see them sitting together, scripts in hand when I walked by her house. They enjoyed acting, but they enjoyed each other's company more."

Ruby stared at her empty coffee cup, trying to think if there was anything else she needed to ask. A burst of cheerful voices came from the hallway, and she stood up and handed Harvey a card. "You've been very helpful. If you can think of anything else…"

"If I do, you'll be the first person I call."

"I like him," Ruby said once they were outside the theater.

"Which means you think he's credible?" Jeremy asked.

"We'll have to run the usual cross-checks, but yeah, my inclination is to give him a stamp of approval. He's got irresistible panache."

Ruby's description of Harvey puzzled him, given what they knew of the guy's reputation.

"His self-confidence attracts people." Ruby shrugged. "I'd go see a show if he's one of the leads."

It figured. Jeremy chastised himself as he climbed into the car's passenger seat. He might have known. Ruby's uncharacteristic actions should have been a signal. Instead of firing back a remark when Harvey had misunderstood the reason for the visit, she'd said nothing and smiled. Jeremy felt silly about his jealousy, wanting Ruby to think of him as highly and as engaging as she did Harvey.

He ignored his urge to compete by listing credentials or telling Ruby stories of cases he'd helped solve in New York. She could dive into his background if she was inclined, and he feared telling tales of his work would only make him sound immature and boastful. Worse, she could research his track record and discover his fall from grace if she wasn't already aware of it.

He pushed the seat belt tongue into the buckle. It made an angry click, which dovetailed with his mood. The longer he thought about the situation, the more his insides churned.

Regain control, slow down.

Ruby climbed into the car and settled behind the steering wheel.

Yes, Jeremy worried about doing a good job and wanted Ruby to like him, just as he'd hoped the deputies and even Commissioner Tom would be impressed with him. But there was no denying there were differences.

He noticed Ruby's behavior more than if she was merely a partner at work. His jaw didn't clench if anyone else paid a lot of attention to the other deputies. His throat didn't close if he saw someone grasp any other deputies' arms. He had to admit Ruby Prescott had awakened emotions and caused reactions in him unlike anyone else. And this bothered Jeremy.

He'd always heard phrases such as "love at first sight" or "made for each other" but doubted their veracity. The idea one person could have a soulmate, a perfect complement, flew in the face of logic. Instant chemical reaction? No way. He'd structured his world around provable facts, and the accumulated data about measurable hormone secretions and pheromones was incomplete.

Jeremy couldn't deny his desire to help Ruby or his need to see her daily, despite the small amount of time they'd known each other. But his career path didn't include a permanent stay in Tinker. And he wasn't sure his interest in her would be reciprocated. No, it was better to keep his feelings to himself and tread as carefully as if he were asked to analyze a crime scene.

The next two weeks flew by. When Ruby drove to Denver for a three-day business trip, Jeremy partnered with Deputy Bill. Their days included investigating a prowler who turned out to be an opossum that had busted through a loose screen in the complainant's back door and sorting out a traffic snarl caused by a stubborn mule deer that occupied the center of the main thoroughfare.

Tasked with gathering more information about Billy Jenkins, Jeremy examined yearbooks, available courtesy of Lucille, spoke to as many of Billy's old acquaintances as he could locate and completed a search of the newspaper archives in order to assemble as full a picture as possible of the deceased suspect.

When he wasn't working, Jeremy, who'd signed a short-term lease for a small house on the outskirts of town, busied himself haunting the store next to the Tinker Museum. He struck up a friendship with the museum docent, who helped him select pieces of furniture to transform the house into a home.

Jeremy considered his church attendance with Ruby to be the highlight of the week. The pastor preached about the value of community, citing several excerpts from Proverbs to illustrate the sermon. He and Ruby listened and then prayed together, and by the end of the service, Jeremy's confidence had swelled so much he suggested lunch and then a walk around Casper Lake to extend their leisure time together.

His concern about events at the district attorney's office in New York lessened the longer Jeremy remained in Tinker, and he began to question his assumption that he needed to return there in a few months. The priorities in his world were changing.

Jeremy joined Ruby to review the evidence in what the local newspaper had dubbed the "Lost Bones Found" affair late on the following Friday afternoon. They stared at the diagrams of the theater. They examined the photographs taken of the theater prop room a second and then a third time. Ruby shared that the forensic anthropologist in Denver had confirmed the piece of jewelry found in the trunk full of bones was an earring from a now defunct gold manufacturer popular at the time.

They took note of what the weight of the trunk would be with Eleanor's body inside, and concluded any of the suspects had the strength to lift it onto the lower shelf, where it had remained for fifty years.

"Ruby, I gotta say I admire your bravery. Don't know how I'd handle being assaulted by a skeleton."

"Well, fifty years is a long time. Once I got over the initial shock, it wasn't so bad. Just dust, a tarnished earring, remnants of a scarf, the bones and a musty smell."

He reported his findings about Billy Jenkins to Ruby. "I gathered most of my information from newspaper articles. The people I spoke to did remember the accident that caused his death, but not much else. It wasn't a suicide. A drunk driver struck Billy." He shuffled some printouts. "He was a teenager who, according to high school yearbooks, joined a couple of clubs, including drama, maintained average grades and dated Anna Jones exclusively."

"Do you think he's involved in the murder?"

"No." Jeremy shook his head. "None of the information I found even hinted at a motive for him to kill anyone."

Ruby got out of her chair and began to pace around the table. "I agree. Strike Billy off the list."

"Next."

"Harvey. I know you aren't a fan, but I found

him credible. Huge ego, yes. Self-absorbed, definitely. But my gut tells me he isn't involved in the homicide. I think he's telling the truth."

"Do you always go with your gut?"

"I do."

Those two simple words packed a punch that almost bowled Jeremy over. Ruby believed in herself, in her intuition. He needed to assemble facts gathered from outside sources and verify every conclusion. And try as he might, he couldn't recall a time when he'd trusted himself enough to act on inclination by itself. He gazed at Ruby with a mixture of admiration and envy.

"I'll admit I don't like him, but I don't see Harvey as a murderer either," Jeremy said at last, "which leaves us with the girls."

"It does indeed."

"I got the distinct impression Anna resented being questioned."

"Yeah, but that's a common reaction. Some people don't like me." Ruby chuckled. "Part of the territory."

"You're thinking her attitude toward us and history of disagreeing with the victim provides Anna with a motive. An argument gone too far. In the heat of the moment, Anna pushes or hits Eleanor, accidentally killing her, panics and stuffs her in the trunk. Her cover story that she was with Billy and nowhere near the theater can't be checked."

"Yep." Ruby nodded.

"What about Lucille?"

"We have a problem. There's no motive."

"That we know of, but maybe we don't know. As Lucille said when we met her, we don't have to prove motive."

"Lucille cooperated and she's your number one fan." Ruby grinned. "She even gave you some of her bird journals. Don't you trust her?"

"I don't know, but her behavior after Eleanor's disappearance interests me. It's weird. Other people commented on it, even Harvey."

"Especially Harvey. And he concluded she was depressed."

"Yes, but her alibi, offered freely, can't be substantiated." Jeremy frowned.

"The sticking point for me is why Lucille would put herself in such close proximity to Eleanor on the day she disappeared. She could have denied being at the theater that day. Who would know the difference?"

"Some criminals deliberately insert themselves into the crime scene. Besides Lucille may be afraid someone saw her that day with Eleanor, so she provided herself an alibi by using the dead guy."

Ruby grimaced. "We've reached a stalemate. I like Anna for the murder, and you seem to be leaning toward Lucille. But whoever the murderer is, they've had half a century to create a plausible story."

"It's going to come down to linking one of the ladies to hard evidence."

Ruby sat back down. "Exactly. Tomorrow I want to show these photographs to Stanley Kell, our retired coroner, and pick his brain. If anyone's an expert at digging out the truth, he is."

TWELVE

The call came close to midnight. Jeremy jolted awake and reached for the phone. His stomach clenched and he braced himself for bad news. No one called so late in the evening unless it was an emergency. Had something happened to Ruby?

Commissioner Tom Ewan identified himself, but Jeremy would have recognized the brash tone of voice even though they'd only interacted on the morning he arrived in Tinker.

What can't wait till tomorrow?

Commissioner Tom skipped the preliminaries. "I need to see you in my office tonight. What I want to discuss won't wait until morning."

"Give me fifteen." Jeremy considered throwing a coat over his pajamas, then decided against it. He agreed with Harvey it was all about the look, and he wanted to stay on the good side of the commissioner, so he pulled on a pair of jeans and threw on a flannel shirt before grabbing his jacket and heading out. The moon provided enough illumination to allow Jeremy to see his breath come out in puffs in the chill November air.

This summons reminded him of late nights in New York, when his supervisor had called him in for clandestine meetings after his career started to tank. The thought of recurring secret meetings depressed him as unwanted images of past history flooded his memory.

"You made good time. I count that in your favor."

Commissioner Tom spoke as if he were rating him.

Jeremy disliked the man's arrogant attitude.

"Say, did you catch the buzz I created for you on *News at Nine*? Great job, if I do say so myself."

"I did. Thank you." Jeremy could be adept at not speaking his mind, and he believed it prudent to stay silent at least until he could determine the direction of the conversation.

"Well, I didn't call you here to talk about the stellar job I've been doing. I'm interested in your take on your job."

"It's been a good three weeks. The personnel are supportive. We're working well as a team. It's a change of pace for me since I get out in the field a lot more, but I can't complain. More work with animals too." Jeremy smiled as he recalled the opossum and the mule deer escapades. Even his brush with the great horned owl hadn't been a total failure.

"I'm glad. When I spoke to your old supervisor tonight I told him you'd learned the ropes faster than I expected and seemed to be fitting in, which is good because I have some bad news."

"Oh?"

"You remember the job opening New York promised to hold for you? Well, they've moved on and left you in their dust."

"What?"

"They've got a new golden boy. You're out, he's in."

Jeremy's mouth gaped open.

"Now look, son, you had to expect something like this would happen. New York never sleeps. It's a hungry machine that gobbles people up and spits them out faster than a spittlebug sucks plant juice. You lived there, you know how it works. The brass, the media, the town—everyone needs a hero. Up until a few months ago, you fit the bill. But you can't fill it in absentia. So your supervisor groomed someone else to step up. It's nothing personal."

Nothing personal? Just my livelihood, my career, my life.

"Your supervisor's an old friend, so when questions about the accuracy of your profiles came up, I suggested you get transferred here to solve our little problem. Well, not so little. It's been on us like a tick on a dog."

"I understand."

"Sounded like a win-win. New York gets you out of the hot seat and we get a super tool to solve our crime crisis. But the phone call I received tonight changed things. What this means is you're mine." Commissioner Tom jabbed his finger at himself and then pointed it at Jeremy. "So what I need from you right now is a progress report. How's the work on the serial burglar progressing?"

Jeremy hesitated. He and Ruby had been focused on the murder, which left little time for anything else. But it wasn't the answer Commissioner Tom wanted to hear.

"I've assembled tools to examine the problem, including the notes and reports about the previous incidents, birding journals to cross-check their feeding behavior with patterns of human foot traffic, maps so the locations of criminal activity can be pinpointed and lists of stolen articles and pawn shops in and around Tinker."

"Birding journals? You don't say."

Jeremy ignored the sarcasm.

"We've been working our tails off, but we gotta take time to sleep."

"Are you saying you don't have enough time to catch a burglar? Do you understand how ineffective it makes you look? And if you look ineffective, I look ineffective. I'm on the line here. I put myself on the *News at Nine* to tout your skills. There's an election on the horizon and your behavior or lack of it can make me look like a fool."

"A murder's taken up a lot of our time."

"A fifty-plus-year-old murder. Pardon me if I can't see the urgency. There's a good chance the perp is dead, and even if they're still with us, what danger could an octogenarian killer pose?"

"How would it look if we turned a blind eye to a crime because of its history? The sheriff can't send the message that doing a crime's okay, so long as you aren't caught within, say, ten years of its commission."

"Of course not, but this serial burglar's a danger to people and their businesses right now. It's a threatening cloud hanging over Tinker. People who vote in the upcoming election are upset, and that upsets me."

"I'll get on it tomorrow," Jeremy said.

"See that you do."

Jeremy got up to leave.

"One more thing. With election activity ramping up, Ruby Prescott is one of the biggest thorns in my side. She and I have a tradition of animosity that precedes your arrival in Tinker, but you can take my word for it, the lady's got to go. You may be wondering about your role in local politics. Think of yourself as my advisor, my private advisor."

"Come again?"

"You work closely with her. Over time, you'll gain her trust. Already you've won over a number of key people in Tinker, thanks to that media coverage. What I need to know about is a weakness, something that impacts her ability to continue to work as the sheriff."

Jeremy couldn't believe his ears.

"I've looked into her background. The information I've gathered would as likely elicit a sympathy vote in her favor as discredit her. But I know there's got to be a skeleton in the closet, a secret that would tarnish her reputation or reflect on her ability to do the job if it became known. That's what I want."

Jeremy frowned.

"Now, I know what you're thinking. That I'm all about me. But I take care of my people. And once she's gone, who better to become sheriff elect than you? Together we'll get her." Commissioner Tom smirked.

Jeremy said nothing as he pushed his chair back and stood, speechless. If the good commissioner had his way, Jeremy would be transformed from a man seeking vindication into a mole on a leash held by one of the kingpins in town. He turned on his heel and left the room.

Jeremy's head spun. Any chance of redemption was lost. Now his supervisor in New York would never realize the overzealous detectives who applied his profile to an innocent man had used it incorrectly.

He sat in his car, perched near the edge of a cliff

overlooking the south end of Casper Lake, bowed
his head and said a short prayer. He remembered
some advice from a friend who'd accepted Jesus
into his life. Rejection was God's way of providing a path for future acceptance. But he didn't
feel all that close to God right now, and his current situation sure didn't feel like an opportunity.

Commissioner Tom had piled a lot on his plate.
Jeremy tried to wrap his mind around the fact he
was stuck in this tumbleweed town with limited
career opportunities. He considered phoning his
old supervisor in New York to verify what Commissioner Tom had told him and pulled his cell
phone out of his pocket only to set it down without punching in the number. No. There was no
point putting any more energy into a lost cause.

And what was this attack on Ruby?

It'd been three weeks, and despite his better
judgment, he'd become emotionally involved.
Hers was the last face he saw before bed and the
first thing he thought about upon awakening. He
resented being dragged into local politics to dig
up dirt about anyone, especially Ruby.

Jeremy grimaced. He'd been shoved into a corner. There had to be a way to turn this around.
He couldn't see it now, but maybe his friend was
right. With God's help, he could forge a new path.

He'd promised the commissioner he would work
on the burglary, and Jeremy was a man of his
word. As for spying and discovering secrets, he

hadn't said a thing. In fact, the longer he thought about it, the angrier he became.

Ruby sometimes struck him as prickly, but Jeremy thought this stemmed from a fear of becoming too open. She encouraged everyone around her and even reached out and forgave him, no matter how much frustration his actions created.

He remembered her face at Rock Garden Park, when he tried to breach the gate. It had been pinched with exasperation, but underneath he could sense compassion, and he couldn't help but wonder if she thought about him the way he did about her. *Whoa.* Where was this coming from?

You'd better put on the brakes, Mr. Jeremy Lawson.

He didn't intend to betray this woman, but neither could he afford to get more involved.

Jeremy started the car, mind still whirring, and turned onto Main Street, home to a row of small tourist shops shut down for the night. The sidewalk was empty save for a lone pedestrian who reached a corner and disappeared from sight. The only vehicle he could see was parked two blocks away under a streetlight. It was gray, with its wheels snug against the curb.

He kept his window cranked half open, wide enough for him to tip his head and look skyward. No clouds, which made stargazing a possibility if he'd been in the mood. He wasn't. It felt as if he'd dropped into a ghost town.

Eager to get back to bed, Jeremy decided to take the direct route home, down Center Street to Ponderosa. Nothing stirred, but as he signaled to turn onto Ponderosa, he glanced in the rearview mirror and stiffened. He could just make out the headlights of the gray car now half a block behind.

Was someone following him? Jeremy began to take short breaths. The goose bumps forming on his arms made the hair stand up straight.

He pressed the gas pedal, then slammed on the brakes. The other car mimicked his actions, keeping the same distance between them.

He swung the wheel hard left and cut through a lane. Turned right onto Pacific Avenue, pulled into a driveway, killed the lights and ducked.

Who was driving the other vehicle? Jeremy began to run through the possibilities. Commissioner Tom, hoping to keep tabs on him? The murderer wanting to monitor his movements? The serial burglar?

Jeremy waited until the gray car drove slowly into sight. As it passed, he leaned forward to try to see the letters of the mud-caked license but couldn't. All he could make out of the driver was a head covered by a cap pulled low.

Another ten minutes ticked by. Maybe it was his imagination running wild. After all, the commissioner's call had interrupted his sleep. Time to get some rest. He switched on the ignition. The night was over.

* * *

The next morning, Jeremy drove to work intending to pore over the birding journals. But he couldn't shake a deep sense of foreboding. He squinted as he deciphered the handwritten entries. The looped cursive style of penmanship slowed his progress, but by the end of an hour, he determined someone had disturbed a flock of American robins nesting around the theater for three consecutive days prior to the burglary. No doubt about it. This was no spur-of-the-moment prowler. Jeremy concluded the burglar had focused on the theater and planned the crime in advance.

He set the journals aside when Ruby arrived.

"I have news," she announced as she came through the door. "Someone, likely our burglar, broke into Freida's Souvenir Shop overnight."

"Freida's on Main Street?" Jeremy asked. He felt a sinking sensation in his stomach.

"Yes." Ruby's narrowed eyes intensified her grim expression. "This crime fits into the same pattern as the others. Why?"

"Because I had to go out late last night and was followed when I drove down Main."

Ruby's eyes widened. "You weren't hurt, were you?"

"Creeped out is all."

He heard concern in her voice, a concern that belied another emotion. *She cares about me. She really cares about me.* He would need time to process it all.

"I'm relieved. If it happens again or you ever need to talk…" Her words trailed off.

Jeremy kept his voice even. "I chalked it up to my overactive imagination, but maybe it was our burglar wanting to make sure the area was clear before he struck."

"Seems likely," Ruby agreed. "I'm relieved you're okay." She patted his arm.

"We heading over there next?"

"No, I've already dispatched Deputy Martinez to do the processing. I'd rather we concentrate on the homicide and interview my go-to expert on crime scene analysis." Ruby checked her phone and spoke briefly to Janice before indicating he should follow.

They hopped into her SUV. "I'll give you the condensed biography of Stanley Kell," she said as she directed the car north on Pine Ridge Road. "Originally an import from Tulsa, Stanley set up shop as one of four general practitioners but developed a specialty for investigating and certifying deaths. Tinker is in a coroner state, meaning our coroner is elected. The certification, while not necessary, helped, but it was Stanley's popularity in and around the Tinker region that pushed him over the top in every election."

"Okay, I can tell from your tone of voice there's a catch."

"Can't get anything by you." Ruby smiled. "There is indeed. Elected officials in Tinker can't serve more than three consecutive terms, although some exceptions are permitted. Stanley applied for an exception to run in our last election, but it wasn't granted. He was forced to retire, and he didn't take it well, even though he can run for the position again in the next election."

"So, I'm to look forward to an interview with a grumpy, resentful guy?"

"Nope. I'd expect Stanley to respond to our inquiries with enthusiasm. He'll be complimented by our respect for his expertise."

"You have a lot of faith in him."

"I do." Ruby nodded. "He's meticulous, one of those guys who'd spot a grain of grit on a beach of white sand. And I've always enjoyed his sense of humor, though I haven't spoken to him since the last election."

"Sounds like a great guy."

"He is. And every day of the week at this time in the morning, you can find him sweating it out on the squash court."

THIRTEEN

"Believe it or not, this is my first visit here." Ruby half turned to catch Jeremy's reaction to the ten-foot-high ceilings and the perfectly centered crystal chandelier that graced the foyer of the Tinker Squash Facility.

"Takes your breath away, but it intimidates me," Jeremy admitted.

"I can't see forking over a year's salary for a one-year membership," Ruby agreed as she approached the twentysomething girl standing behind the intake counter.

The receptionist continued to stare at her ledger and didn't look up. "You folks are early for the tour."

"We're not here for a tour," Ruby said as she showed the girl her identification. "We plan to meet Stanley Kell. I understand he's a member."

"Oh, yes, Mr. Kell." The girl's smile reached her eyes. "He's one of my favorites, a true gentleman." She leaned forward conspiratorially. "Some of our members can be snooty," she whispered, "but not Mr. Kell. He always tells me to call him Stanley, but I can't seem to bring myself to do it. He's so refined."

"I believe he's expecting us."

"He may be, but right now he's playing on court five. He should be free in another twenty minutes. I know because someone else has the same court booked for eleven. You can wait in our café or watch the match from our viewing gallery on the second floor."

"Elevator or stairs?" Jeremy asked.

"Stairs. The exercise never hurts."

As Ruby climbed, she thought about how her estimation of Jeremy had changed. Although she'd resented his assignment to Tinker at first, she had grown accustomed to his company when she responded to calls, examined crime scenes or interviewed people. *Accustomed* was an inadequate word, she realized. Ruby looked forward to her shifts more than she had in the past three years.

Did this make her one of the multitude of Tinker fans who merely reacted to his superhero appearance? Nope. The longer she worked alongside Jeremy, the more she grew to depend on his intellect, stability and reliability.

She still became irked when he interrupted her or talked nonstop about available software programs when, through his comments, he implied the sheriff's office was a second-class sister to police forces in larger metropolitan areas. But he didn't engage in these behaviors as often anymore, which probably corresponded with his increased familiarity with the station and town.

Ruby remembered the brush of his arm against hers when they both reached for the same report. She could bask in that moment of shared warmth forever. How she wished to know what it felt like to be in his arms, drawing her close. Ruby quickly dismissed these thoughts in favor of doing something practical and began to plan her upcoming interview with Stanley.

The viewing gallery, a tiled aisle that ran the length of three squash courts sat a story above the rooms. Spectators looked down at the players through a heavy, acrylic safety wall. Ruby recognized Stanley playing in the middle court and pointed him out to Jeremy.

"He may be midfifties in age, but he's a teenager in agility," she said as they watched Stanley smash the ball against the wall, then sidestep, bend his knees and pivot on his right foot, ready to intercept his opponent's next shot.

"His partner's not too shabby either," Jeremy said.

"True, but he's half Stanley's age. I'm impressed."

Ruby stared down but suddenly stopped speaking. Her heart raced, her grip on the handrail intensified until her knuckles ached. As her vision blurred, she tried to reach up to wipe her eyes, but her muscles wouldn't respond to commands. She couldn't release her hands from the rails.

The memory, like a movie, played out in front of her. It was night and Ruby was driving. She threaded the car through the bluffs that formed the western boundary of Tinker. Her husband, Adam, snoozed in the passenger seat, a side effect of taking his migraine medicine earlier that evening.

Torrential rain hammered the windshield. Ruby swerved, took a corner too wide and then jammed on the brakes. Tires squealed. The car shuddered to a stop, straddling the center line.

Ruby didn't panic. Instead, she took slow, deep breaths and looked over at Adam. He barely stirred, despite the abrupt movement of the car.

The pounding rain continued. A curve in the road loomed large in front of her, obscuring her visibility. They didn't have that far left to go. She willed her hands to stay steady and tried to start the car again, but the engine wouldn't catch. They needed to get to the side of the road and call 911. A blast of wind came up through the valley, rocking the car.

She unlocked the door, unfastened her seat belt and stepped out into the deluge. The rain drilled into her, plastering her hair to her skull, chilling her to the bone.

Ruby sprinted around the front of the car to the passenger side to help Adam from the car. Her muscles ached as she tried to yank and wrestle him out of the seat.

Adam, you have to wake up. But he didn't move a muscle.

The noise of a motor and of gears grinding forced her to look up. Round the curve came two large headlights, piercing the rain and fog.

A bus was hurtling toward them.

At the last second, it swerved to avoid the collision but didn't miss them entirely. Ruby, splayed against the rock wall, watched as the bus sent their car smashing into the cliff face, before shuddering to a stop a short distance away.

The car's passenger side was all but destroyed. She ran as fast as she could to it. Adam's bloody, twisted face and vacant stare were the last memories she had of that day.

Her guttural cry of anguish forced her back to the present. Ruby sank to her knees, her death grip on the handrail unchanged.

Jeremy bent down and held her fast.

His voice was soothing, gentle.

"You are not alone, I'm here. It's okay," he said over and over again.

She released her hands and let her arms fall.

"I'm sorry."

"No. You need to rest."

After a few minutes, Ruby stopped trembling. Embarrassment replaced terror. This was the first time in a year she'd experienced a full-blown panic attack about the terrible night her husband died.

She'd been treated for survivor's guilt and received therapy to help her cope with triggers that could cause an episode. Ruby had been careful to seek professional help from a psychologist in Denver because she worried about the reaction from the townsfolk of Tinker. Would some people see it as a weakness? Darkness and rain no longer held her hostage, but heights still bothered her. She shuddered at the thought of climbing a ladder but had never expected to react when she looked down from the viewing gallery. Should she explain this to Jeremy?

"Let's get you to the café." His voice cut into her thoughts and she nodded. *Be professional and focus on the task at hand.*

Ruby straightened and let Jeremy lead her to the stairwell. Her legs felt like rubber, but she willed herself to concentrate on descending one stair at a time.

"I'm okay as long as I don't look down." If she said it, maybe it would become the truth.

"You'll be fine." Jeremy's warm tone reassured her.

They settled at a table, and Ruby pretended to study a beverage list. Finally she set it aside. "Jeremy…" she began.

"Don't," he said. "Everyone gets overwhelmed." He reached over and cupped her hand in his. "I don't need details or explanations. Just know I support you."

"Thank you." Ruby bowed her head and prayed. She was grateful for Jeremy's support and God's.

Stanley entered the room. "Hey, guys. Ruby, it's been a while. Jeremy?" Stanley stuck his hand out. "Have you folks ordered yet?"

"We waited for you," Jeremy said.

"They've got a smoothie I live on. I'll get us each one."

As Stanley walked to the counter to place the order, Ruby noticed a slight limp. "Hurt your foot in the match?" she asked when he returned to the table with their drinks.

"What? Oh, that, no, I'm fine. I may stumble around the court, but so long as I keep winning matches, I'm happy." He smiled. "Now, you're here to pick my brain."

"Yes." Still recovering from the panic attack, Ruby's hands trembled as she spread the crime scene photographs on the table. A wave of fatigue gripped her.

Jeremy reached out and straightened the photos, a movement that Ruby interpreted as a nonverbal sign he would take over the questioning. Ruby shifted back in her chair and closed her eyes a moment.

Stanley began methodically picking up and studying each picture in turn. "These from the theater where the skeleton was found?"

"Affirmative."

Stanley held out a photo. "What do we have here, remnants of fabric on the bones?"

Jeremy studied the picture for a minute. "Yes."

"If the person in the trunk was clothed, it's less likely they were sexually assaulted," Stanley said.

"Right. What about the scarf?"

"What's left of it doesn't look distinctive, but you may be able to link it to someone."

"Like a signature scarf."

"Exactly. Oh, this one's interesting." Stanley held up a photo of jewelry found in the trunk and squinted. "Looks like a signature piece. I'd say pink sapphire set in gold, probably custom made."

"Is that significant?" Jeremy asked.

"Could be. There may be a manufacturer's seal, microscopic, of course, stamped on the back of the earring, but I can't tell from a picture."

"It's currently with the pathologist," Jeremy confirmed.

"When it's released, check for the stamp. If the jeweler's still in business, you might get a line on the buyer. Gold is too expensive to be used as a theater prop, so it likely belongs to the victim or the perp."

Stanley continued to sift through the photographs and stopped when he reached one that included Ruby. "Tinker's lucky to have you," he said, firmly.

She smiled. "I appreciate that, Stanley."

Stanley continued to thumb through the pictures, then looked up. "Good job, everyone." He handed the photos back to Ruby and took a long pull of his smoothie.

Ruby glanced at her watch. She only had a gulp of her smoothie left but still didn't trust her legs to work seamlessly and decided to stretch out the meeting. Besides, it was her chance to buttonhole Stanley. "Are you planning on running in the next election?" she asked.

"Count on it."

"You haven't enjoyed your retirement?"

"Forced retirement. You know the story. Bureaucracy. Egos. I've been bored silly these last three and a half years, so, yes, I'm running in the next election."

Ruby chewed on her upper lip. "I'd have thought entering triathlons would keep you busy."

"If there were more, maybe you'd be right. But two triathlons a year does not an athletic hobby make. As it is, my training schedule stays the same whether or not I work full time. No, I'm looking forward to my election victory for two reasons. First, I feel a strong sense of duty. And second, I want to see the look on Tom Ewan's face when I'm declared the coroner again."

"Commissioner Tom Ewan?" Jeremy asked. "We've met several times. I wonder about him."

"Wonder no more. I got inside information that he was the only person who voted against the exception to enable me to run in the last election. Apparently I angered him when I refused to vote in favor of his goofy scheme to outfit every homeowner with a security camera—and at the taxpayer's expense. Funny that he had a minority ownership in a similar business. But I saw his suggestion as unnecessary tactic, so he torpedoed my career."

"It's not that there's anything wrong with the current coroner," Ruby said, "but you'll have the edge, Stanley."

"I know it. And am I correct when I assume you will be running for sheriff again, my dear?"

"Yes, but I lack your confidence, Stanley. I've got admirers, but there are always the naysayers. And I'd like to be able to point to a clean track record, which puts pressure on me to solve the homicide and the serial burglaries."

"Ruby, you're a woman of many talents. I'm sure you'll arrest the murderer in due course. As for the burglaries, it's always possible the situation will sort itself out on its own. And if it doesn't, remember, nobody expects perfection."

FOURTEEN

"How many cemeteries are there in Tinker?"

Ruby put on a pair of sunglasses, pulled a map out of the dashboard and pretended to study it before answering. "Four."

"And where's the GPS when you need it?"

"It'd compete with incoming radio calls. Remember, we're law and order."

Jeremy rolled his eyes. "How difficult can locating one graveyard be? I know. Let's roll back history. I'll pull over and we can change seats. You drive."

"Nope. You're doing fine."

Jeremy glanced sideways. Ruby sat back in the passenger seat, arms relaxed, hands in her lap, struggling to keep her mouth from curling up into a smile. A quarter of a mile and one long hill later, row upon row of tombstones came into view.

"I think we're here." Jeremy turned into the church driveway just as Pastor Hank's son, Reverend Cecil Miller, stepped outside the building.

"Thanks for coming so promptly," he said.

"You called about a grave." Ruby adjusted her sunglasses.

"Yes. Come with me, please. It's the strangest thing, about grave markers."

They followed the reverend, who led them to a cluster of tombstones in the southwest corner of the grounds. Jeremy could see two gray granite stones engraved with the surname Costell.

"Two stones, one to mark the passing of the parents and the second, I presume, to mark the eventual grave of the loving daughter, Eleanor."

"Not an unusual practice," Ruby said.

"Normally I'd agree, but one of my parishioners brought up Eleanor's marker to me recently. Since Eleanor's name has become front page news, this piqued my curiosity so I made some inquiries."

"Are you embarking on a second career as a detective?" Ruby's eyes crinkled with pleasure.

"Hardly. But once you get something in your head, well, you know how it is."

"I do," Ruby agreed.

"I contacted Crispin Monuments. The Costell arrangements were prepaid some years before they died. But someone else bought the stone for Eleanor three years after the parents passed."

Ruby and Jeremy looked at each other, momentarily dumbfounded. "Who?"

"Anna Jones."

* * *

"I have no idea what you're talking about." Anna curled her lips and wrinkled her nose as if reacting to a bad smell. "I never bought Eleanor Costell a tombstone. Why would I? I haven't even bought one for myself."

"May we come inside?" Jeremy asked.

He and Ruby stood on the doorstep of Anna's modest home, a Craftsman bungalow nestled in the Black Hills, a small community just outside of Tinker.

"Why? So you can treat me like some sort of criminal? I'd hate to have you overstay your welcome."

"Neighbors." Jeremy could see someone peeking out from behind a curtain in the house across the street.

"The neighbors knew you were here the moment you pulled alongside the curb. They can speculate as much as the day is long. I don't have to talk to you, and I certainly don't intend to invite you into my home."

As Anna moved to shut the door, Jeremy quickly said, "A representative of Crispin Monuments advised us that you're the recorded purchaser of a grave marker for Eleanor Costell."

"They're wrong. And if their recordkeeping is that unreliable, people would be well advised not to use them for funeral arrangements. Now, if you'll excuse me." Anna sniffed before she slammed the door.

* * *

"That didn't go well." Jeremy frowned.

"I disagree. Outright denials are the sheriff's best friend. I love it when a person commits themselves without reservation. Then, if we find contradictory evidence, we can use it to shore up our case against them."

"Is she lying?"

Ruby tapped her cheek. "I don't know, but I do think we can safely narrow the suspect pool to Anna or Lucille."

Jeremy looked down the well-groomed street. "Both ladies could afford to buy the gravestone, although it still behooves me to ask why anyone would have bought it in the first place."

"Behooves? It's come to that, has it?" Ruby grinned. "Next you'll expect me to talk about a malefactress. Anyway, to answer your question, one word—guilt. Whoever committed the murder felt guilty, likely still does. They know Eleanor is dead. They also knew with her parents gone, no one was left to take care of burial details. If they have a shred of decency or any regret about causing Eleanor's death, it's the least they could do."

"An attempt to make amends? Okay. So they're overcome with remorse, but they also realize their actions make them look suspicious, hence the skullduggery."

"And there's plenty of skullduggery to go around in this case." Ruby smiled.

Now outside the quiet community, Jeremy steered the car east to Cumber Way, then onto Pike's Pass. He pulled into the parking lot of Rock Garden Park. "At least today it's open," he quipped.

Jeremy pointed to an outcrop. "Let's walk."

After a quarter of a mile, they stopped and rested on a bench at the Mesa Road Overlook. The Kissing Camels rose to their west. The setting sun reflected off the formation, its glow encircled him, Ruby and the surrounding red sandstone rocks.

Ruby spoke softly. "It must be horrible keeping a secret when you know one wrong step spells exposure."

"It's gotta be a heavy burden." Jeremy thought about Anna and Lucille, one of them forced to live for decades with the knowledge they'd taken a life. Anna's defensive belligerence contrasted with Lucille's efforts to cooperate and ingratiate herself to anyone investigating the murder, but either reaction could mask a terrible secret.

Heavy burden? Yes. He knew all too well what it meant to keep a secret and always be on guard. He constantly caught himself being careful to monitor what he said and what he did, lest he slip.

"Magnificent, isn't it?" Ruby touched his arm and indicated the Kissing Camels.

"A natural embodiment of love," he agreed, his voice hushed.

Had he gone too far? Jeremy stole a look at Ruby. She gave no indication of discomfort. In fact, she was the most beautiful woman he'd ever seen. But it was her heart that really spoke to him. For the first time, he was truly grateful that he was here in Tinker. It had led him to her. He wondered again about what it would be like to share a closeness with her.

Sunset at Rock Garden Park—the perfect backdrop for a first kiss. He longed to tell Ruby how much she meant to him. But the realization he hadn't divulged how one of his profiles had led to a man being unfairly arrested crashed into his thoughts and chased away any hint of romance. If there was any relationship to pursue, it had to be based on full disclosure. It wasn't fair to expect Ruby to offer herself to a shadow of a man.

She needed to be told his arrival at Tinker had more to do with a single mistake and wrongful accusations about his work and less with any acumen he brought to the table. That Commissioner Tom understood all of this gave him leverage over Jeremy.

What if he told Ruby the truth and she thought less of him? But what if someone else, a news reporter like Bess Trundle, dug up his history and disclosed his secret? He sighed, aware of the irony of his situation. Here he sat surrounded by rock and ruminated about being stuck in a hard place.

"I'll give you a penny for your thoughts," Ruby said.

This was the moment. He could feel it in his bones. Jeremy took a deep breath.

"Commissioner Tom built me up pretty good on television," he began.

"You must be pleased."

"Not exactly." Jeremy took a second deep breath. "The news clip cast me in a false light," he blurted.

"Hey," Ruby interrupted, "you know we were kidding you when everyone saw the clip together at the office?"

"I know."

"When I say 'kidding,' I don't mean you aren't a good guy, but it was fun to see you squirm."

"I get that. But hear me out. Commissioner Tom went to great lengths to sell me to the public, and to you, as some sort of secret weapon. Not only did he exaggerate about my abilities at the expense of good people already in the sheriff's office, he failed to disclose why my transfer took place."

Ruby stared at him, but he could sense sympathy behind her eyes. "Does that matter?"

"I think so." Jeremy swallowed. "A year ago I was one of the top people in New York's Forensic Operations Department. All that changed when I provided a profile to the detectives working a homicide."

"Go on," Ruby said.

"They already had a strong suspect. The investigating officers used my profile in an overzealous search for specific evidence, although I insisted it only provided general parameters and was better used to rule people out. No one listened. But later, after a wrongful conviction, people made a lot of accusations."

"Oh no."

"The media claimed evidence may have been manufactured. Someone else suggested witnesses had been unduly influenced. It became a real circus. Then people focused on the profile. The media blamed me for deliberately creating a tool which pinpointed a guy who'd caused me a lot of trouble. People higher up in my department concluded I was the problem. When my supervisors and the union stayed quiet, their silence was interpreted as a tacit agreement with my accusers."

Ruby harrumphed. "Sounds like they needed a scapegoat. They must not have known you very well. I've only worked with you a month, and I'd guarantee you'd never misuse your knowledge in that way."

"Thanks." The fact Ruby sided with him filled him with hope. But when she heard the rest, he doubted she'd remain as forgiving. He gazed skyward. *Lord, give me courage to continue.*

"Commissioner Tom put a positive spin on my transfer. But I was given just four hours to pack and head out to Tinker."

"What would've happened if you'd refused?"

"When you get smeared in New York, you can kiss your career goodbye, and that's just the beginning. There was talk of a formal suspension and investigation. I could've been sued or even charged criminally, so my supervisor took remedial steps."

"And those remedial steps involved Commis-sioner Tom," Ruby said.

"Exactly." Jeremy hung his head momentarily. "The last thing my supervisor said was to hang in there. If I kept my head down in Tinker, he'd handle things, and I could return to my old job in six months."

Jeremy saw Ruby's body stiffen as he continued to talk. Now she moved away from him slightly. "So, you're stuck in Tinker temporarily."

A statement not a question.

"Originally, yes." There was no sense in deny-ing it. And there was no mistaking the expres-sion on Ruby's face, a mixture of disappointment and defeat.

"Why are you telling me this now?"

Jeremy noticed her upper lip curl slightly when she asked the question.

"I'm worried someone will dig into my place-ment in Tinker. I didn't want you to find out about this from someone else."

Ruby frowned. "And this impacts me how?"

"It could lower your opinion of me. It might hurt your chances for reelection too. What if you come out officially supporting me and I go down in flames? What if someone thinks my transfer wasn't about me being good for Tinker as much as Commissioner Tom doing a favor to ingratiate himself with New York?"

"I think you're wrong about the impact of this

secret on me. I support all of my team, no exceptions. And if I had no influence on or details about your appointment, and I didn't, suggestions of wrongdoing can't tarnish me, only Commissioner Tom, which means they'll never see the light of day."

Relief flooded through Jeremy. Ruby's confidence lessened the worry that his past could hurt her. He'd divulged his secret, and the ground was still solid under his feet. Jeremy thought about what to say next.

Should he tell her how, over the past month, thoughts of her affected his every decision? Explain how his attachment to her had grown? He wanted, no, needed to know if she felt this connection. The fact she was his boss mattered less than his need to share his hopes and dreams with this woman, now and forever.

Jeremy leaned forward and counted the branches still bearing leaves on a frosted scrub oak. He bit his lip and then began to speak. "There was another reason I told you my secret. Over the past month, I've grown attached to the town and to you, Ruby Prescott." He turned sideways on the bench and forced eye contact with Ruby. How he wanted to hear her return the sentiment, utter the words *I've grown attached to you too, Jeremy.*

But Ruby broke eye contact with him and stared at the Kissing Camels.

FIFTEEN

She knew he was waiting and Ruby yearned to echo Jeremy's sentiment. From the moment she'd laid eyes on him, she wrestled with an undeniable attraction, an attraction that triggered her defenses until she pushed him away with brusque comments. Many nights were spent lying sleepless while she tried to banish him from her thoughts. But over time she came to appreciate the care and concern behind his numerous questions and suggestions. To say he awakened a portion of her emotions and a part of her spirit she believed dead would not be mistaken.

Ruby likened them to the two Kissing Camels made of stone, almost touching but forever separated, immobile because of their inherent nature and factors beyond their control. She wanted to reach out to him, to acknowledge what he meant to her. She longed for the chance to become closer but had shunned developing an intimate relationship with anyone since the death of her husband.

There never seemed to be a right time to make that first step.

She had grieved for a year, then spent four years learning to cope with survivor's guilt. A combination of relief and anticipation that she'd finally met someone who could chisel a crack in the wall she'd erected around her heart awakened her hope for the future. But it worried her that this person bore boulders so large they seemed insurmountable. And Jeremy had dropped a lot of information into her lap, information which she needed time to digest.

There was the matter of favoritism. Although she'd brushed off Jeremy's worries that his transfer to Tinker could prove embarrassing, she was concerned. Even if Commissioner Tom succeeded in hiding any impropriety, she wondered if staying her doubts instead of actively investigating the situation increased her complicity in any wrongdoing of the case.

Of course there was always the possibility Jeremy's assessment of the situation was wrong. If everything was on the up-and-up, there was no problem. Except rarely were things that simple. And she knew the danger posed by any real or imagined transgression could affect her chances for reelection.

Jeremy had to know his appearance at the sheriff's office was irregular. No aptitude test or job interview, just another situation thrust upon her. And yet he'd waited a full month before saying anything.

She wondered what bothered her more: the facts of his transfer or his failure to disclose those facts earlier. If he cared for her, why hadn't he trusted her? Could his reluctance to make full disclosure predict behavior she could expect in a romantic relationship? How many other secrets were left for her to unearth?

But the thought that she might also be guilty of withholding information niggled into her consciousness. When panic forced her secret into the open at the squash court, Jeremy's immediate reaction had been to comfort her, not push her away. But there were fundamental differences between the two situations. Ruby's personal fear of heights couldn't compare to possible involvement in an incident of favoritism.

Jeremy's initial attitude toward Tinker didn't bode well either. Coming here had not been a positive choice. When she'd asked him about it at their lunch, he'd said it was time for a change, but the fact that he only intended to stay for six months was new information, information that bothered her.

She was not a woman who engaged in flirtations. Limited involvement for a short time held no appeal. But Jeremy didn't seem to be the type of man to frequent bars or clubs or flit from one woman to another. In fact, she recalled most of his free time in New York was spent at work or with his nephew.

"You mentioned going back to New York five months down the road." She scrutinized his face while she waited for his response.

"I didn't have much say when those plans were made," he replied. "They thrust the timeline on me. But my eyes have been opened a lot in my short time here. I aim to take hold of my future, though what it'll look like, I still can't say for sure."

"What about your job?"

"Here or in New York?"

"Both."

"I'm not sure of my status in New York, but right now life in Tinker appeals to me more than climbing a ladder in the Big Apple."

"A decision to stay in Tinker will impact your income and your career projections." Ruby's shoulders lowered as the tension melted away. Talking about careers seemed safer than discussing the possibility of a romantic entanglement.

"I know. But there are two things I can say. I no longer think of Tinker as a a fallback location to build a future. And I know I want to take our relationship to the next level."

Ruby gazed at the Kissing Camels again and then looked at Jeremy. "I'd like that too," she said at last.

"I've heard of drowning in paperwork, but this is ridiculous." Jeremy could see photographs piled so high on the front counter of the sheriff's office it obscured his view of the deputy behind the desk. He walked over to the tallest stack, lifted a sheet off the top and groaned. An eight by ten image of a man with a strong face, square jaw and deep brown eyes stared back at him. There was no cape.

"Where'd this picture come from?" he asked.

"I took it," Deborah held up her smartphone.

"Practicing our surveillance skills, are we, Deputy Dean?"

"Someone had to do it. We knew you'd never go to the photographer yourself despite the sheriff's promise of an autographed picture to be distributed at the Thanksgiving Festival. Were you hoping we'd forget? I had to do something. The holiday's right around the corner."

"Looks good. How'd you get my autograph?"

"Grabbed it off one of your reports."

"One last question—why so many? There have to be a couple of thousand here."

"Exactly 5,500, but who's counting?"

"The population of Tinker is 4,800, give or take, and that includes every man, woman and child. Can you say 'overkill'?"

"Nah. You'll run out within an hour. Some folks will want two or three. Plus, our Thanksgiving parade and fair attracts people from towns in a thirty-mile radius. Trust me, you are a star, Jeremy Lawson."

"Glad to hear it." Jeremy swept his hair off his

forehead and puffed his chest. He held the pose a full minute before saying, "It's time for this star to head to his desk and get some work done."

Ruby walked through the front office. "Hey, everyone, I'm popping over to Crispin Monuments to get a copy of the record of purchase for our victim's gravestone."

Jeremy looked at the clock beside the window and smiled. He estimated it would take Ruby at least sixty minutes to gather the information from Crispin's, which meant he had a clear hour to produce a profile of the serial burglaries. He'd been brought to Tinker to catch a burglar, and that's what he intended to do.

Jeremy sifted through the papers. Normally he'd have the software available to conduct a spatial analysis of the crime. Not today. He spread a street map of Tinker on his desk and pressed pushpins into the five locations where the burglaries took place, numbering them in order of occurrence.

The first, a long defunct tuberculosis hut, sat on a plateau in the shadow of the Rockies.

He knew many of the tepee-shaped rock structures, with vents around the roof and openings around the base to increase air flow, had been refurbished and were now used for storage or as artist studios, but the targeted hut was one of the few empties left standing in a deserted area the size of a football field.

Jeremy wondered why this ramshackle hut would attract a prowler. There could be nothing of value inside. He leaned back in his chair and thought about its location relative to the other re-invented hut settlements closer to town. Its isolation would appeal, particularly for a beginner burglar who would find avoiding security patrols and gaining entry by scaling the crumpled retaining wall a big enough challenge for their first adventure.

The second target, a building that had housed workers who labored to clear hiking trails on Red Mountain, upped the ante from the burglar's perspective. This location, at the midpoint on an incline, proved difficult to access compared with the first target and marked the farthest-flung point of a security patrol that made regular rounds on a two-hour schedule.

As with the first target, there was little of value inside the structure, and the report stated nothing was taken, but Jeremy could envision the appeal of scaling a path up a moderately steep incline to tackle a break and enter where townsfolk preserved the relic as a testament to Tinker's history. If he put himself in the prowler's shoes, he could imagine the adrenaline rush that would accompany the violation of a treasured space.

The third establishment, a vehicle repair shop, was the burglar's first foray into a working business closed for the evening. With enhanced security, including high fences and cameras that made regular sweeps of the lot, Bernie's Repair posed formidable obstacles for anyone planning a break and enter. But it had been successful. The burglar even took a souvenir, a lug wrench, which could serve as a weapon in addition to being a memento of his transgression.

Jeremy could see a pattern of escalating behavior. Each target built on the last; each demanded a skill set that grew ever more refined.

It was the fourth target, the abandoned theater, that didn't seem to fit the pattern. Located on the edge of town, out of business for fifty years, with little of value inside and no apparent security to breach, Jeremy couldn't see a relationship between this crime and the earlier ones at first. But there had been a major difference. This time, the prowler had almost gotten caught.

He reminded himself that the theater did have a security system: an old woman armed with night vision binoculars. Perhaps the burglar reached the same conclusion and counted on someone watching from the house to call in the burglary.

Jeremy slapped his forehead. That had to be the point. The prowler chose the venue to challenge the sheriff. It seemed silly at first, but when Jeremy took a mental step backward, he could visualize the curriculum for a Burglary 101 course. It was simple. The successful completion of one confidence-building step led to the next.

The last burglary, the one he'd almost inter-rupted, would have been another test in that pro-gression after almost getting caught at the theater.

Jeremy sat back in his chair and rubbed his hands together. Success. The burglar was intel-ligent, with well-developed organizational skills, and was in good physical shape. He chose targets after careful consideration of their elements. And although his analysis didn't tell Jeremy who, it an-swered the question of why.

He could predict two goals of the prowler: to gain skill in his chosen craft and to execute a heist that would prove him superior. Now Jeremy only needed to identify the sixth target, stake it out and arrest the culprit. He bent over the map again to continue his scrutiny.

"This should be easy." Ruby spread the receipt from Crispin Monuments on her desk. "As clear as day, signed by Anna Jones."

"But is it?" said Jeremy.

"What do you mean?" Ruby tipped her head.

"Anna gave you a paper with her particulars when we spoke to her at the library, didn't she?"

"Yeah, I've got it over here." Ruby pulled a small square of paper from a file folder marked with the suspect's name and set it alongside the receipt.

Jeremy squinted. "This is no good. Anna printed her name and contact information. But I can't get around it, the writing looks familiar." He snapped his fingers. "Wait a minute."

He hurried out of the room and came back with two of Lucille's bird ledgers. "Now see? Look. The lowercase 'a' in the signature of Anna and the one in the term 'American Robin' are similar, both formed using a looped cursive style."

"How unique is the handwriting style?"

"It was more popular fifty years ago. At least, that's what my research said. Today, maybe thirty-seven percent of people write in it."

Ruby frowned. "So, since they're about the same age, Anna and Lucille probably both use the looped cursive style."

"Simple." Jeremy snapped his fingers. "Let's send samples from both women with the Crispin receipt to get an analysis."

"I doubt Anna would cooperate and give us a sample. We'd need a subpoena."

"Can you get one?"

"Probably, but I've got a better idea." Ruby hunched over a computer and googled the *Tinker Daily*. "There's an 'It's Your Say' half page in the paper, and guess who's a prolific letter writer?"

"Anna Jones."

"You got it. On my way out, I'll stop by the newspaper office and get a copy of one of her letters from their records."

"A typed letter puts us no further ahead."

"Newspaper policy, all letters to the editor must

be personally signed. This after a huge problem cropped up when one person who claimed to be someone else sent in an inflammatory letter that got published."

"Excuse me." Deborah stuck her head in the door. "Sorry to interrupt, but you've got a phone call, Ruby. I think its Frank Dosser. There's a mini crisis brewing over the final arrangements for the holiday parade."

SIXTEEN

"Yippee. Pie day." Ruby smacked her lips and turned to Jeremy. "Around here we start the Thanksgiving Day celebration with a sampling of Mrs. Sandberg's Palisade peach pies."

"She sure does speak the Thanksgiving language," Deputy Dean agreed as she cut generous portions of the dessert for everyone.

Ruby bowed her head. *Almighty God, on this morning we celebrate the season. We give thanks for our friends and our neighbors. We ask You to keep us safe as we continue on the course You set out for us. Amen.*

As everyone reached for a plate and began to fork bites of the pie into their mouths, Ruby surveyed the group of five capable coworkers. She'd put her life on the line for any of them and knew they'd do the same for her and each other.

Ruby gestured to Desmond. "Say, did Jeb Hancock and Mrs. Sandberg ever get together?"

The deputy grinned. "Since I dropped the hint to Mrs. Sandberg, Jeb hasn't been back to the cells and Mrs. Sandberg's ghosts vacated her premises. I'd say it's a match."

"That's something to give thanks for," Ruby said. "In fact, overall we've had a good year. We can be proud of our closure rate. And I expect our two open cases, the serial burglaries and the murder of Eleanor Costell, will be closed within a month, so let's give ourselves a break from crime, at least for today, and enjoy the festivities."

"Is that an order?" Deputy Deborah's eyes twinkled.

"It is indeed. Now, is everyone ready for the parade?" Ruby put her fork on her plate and set it on the front counter.

Deborah piped up, "I am. Deputies on the four corners of our float, with you and Jeremy in the center waving at the crowd underneath a banner stating our motto, Keeping the Peace to Create Goodwill."

"I can picture it." Jeremy smiled.

"I hate to be a naysayer, but I'm not sure having everyone tied up on the float works." Desmond frowned.

"We haven't had a problem before, presumably because the bad guys are watching the parade with everyone else, but you make a good point," Deborah agreed.

"Why don't we raid our stash of bicycles?" Bill suggested.

"Great solution," Ruby agreed. "The deputies

can form a bicycle squad to ride alongside the float. They'll have more mobility should it be required. Problem solved."

Mayor Dosser designed the parade route to curl along Casper Lake Drive, then head north so the floats and marching bands could finish with a triumphant run along Main Street.

The longstanding tradition that put the mayor at the head of the planning committee gave the incumbent an opportunity to display their creativity and endear them to the electorate. And by the look of it, Frank had outdone himself.

Ruby touched Jeremy's arm. "Let's walk the line," she said.

How she longed to take Jeremy's hand in hers as they strolled down the road and shared reactions to the variety of displays. It had taken five long years, but she'd decided to take a chance and open her heart to him, and on this Thanksgiving Day her emotions threatened to explode. She mouthed a silent prayer.

Ruby thought her inability to save her husband's life on that stormy night sealed the deal, and she'd resigned herself to a life spent with ruminations about her failures. Grateful for a second chance, she made a silent vow to do everything in her power to honor her commitment to form a deeper relationship with Jeremy based on love and respect.

A burst of red caught her eye. Pots of poinsettias

decorated the Senior Center float. Enlarged photographs of several older women around a crafts table and another of seniors practicing yoga poses provided onlookers with a picture of the variety of activities available at the center. Ruby noticed Anna Jones moving methodically around the float watering the plants. Ruby waved when Anna looked in her direction, but instead of acknowledging the greeting, Anna scowled and turned away.

"Hey, there's Harvey Klingshot talking to your friend Stanley Kell," Jeremy said.

The men stood to the side of a float displaying wildlife close-ups and advertising several hunting and fishing lodges in the area. True to form, Harvey sported an attention-grabbing green fedora and punctuated his conversation with grand gestures while Stanley listened, being careful to keep enough distance between them to avoid a possible catastrophe.

"Your friend is drab compared to Harvey."

"Huh. I'd always figured he'd be outfitted in the latest khaki pants and top-of-the-line shirt, being an avid outdoorsman, but come to think of it, I rarely saw him outside the coroner's office, where he always wore a lab coat. It's funny how you can make assumptions about people, but after seeing him in gray and dark blue, drab is an apt description."

"Sheriff Ruby. Jeremy. Hidey-ho. What a lovely day." Lucille bustled over and addressed them both, but Ruby noticed her eyes never left Jeremy's face.

"I can hardly wait to get an autographed headshot after the parade. Maybe you could consider leading a fundraiser by offering yourself as a home security specialist. I'd be one of the highest bidders."

"Now, Lucille, don't you go starting a riot with your suggestions. I'm far too busy fighting crime right now, but maybe once things settle down." Jeremy bowed and clicked his heels before taking Ruby's elbow and steering her toward the end of the line.

The sidewalks were filled with onlookers, many of whom waved flags. Children ran around playing games. The sun shone bright, keeping the temperatures in the high forties. Men and women decked out in chef's hats handed out cups of hot chocolate, and a crowd of people surrounding a Treats for Sale stand grinned and clapped each other on the back. This year the inclusion of walking pumpkins delighted Ruby. The people wearing orange gloves with orange globes covering their head added a comic touch to the festivities.

Ruby ranked Thanksgiving, a time of universal goodwill, her favorite celebration of the year.

"We'd better get to our starting point." Jeremy turned, waited for Ruby to catch up and then began moving toward the front of the line.

The sheriff's float had been positioned two back behind the parade marshal's vehicle, a convertible with a built-in throne that covered the rear seat. He could see the mayor, dressed in a rust-colored suit, patting down his trousers as he readied himself to step into the marshal's chair. *Prosper with Dosser.* This parade certainly conveyed the message Tinker was in good hands with Dosser at its helm.

Jeremy sensed movement in his peripheral vision and turned his head to the left. Nothing to see, but a sense of foreboding lingered. He remembered Ruby's admonition to leave work behind for today and pushed his suspicions away. But he gritted his teeth because he couldn't shake an inexplicable apprehension that something wasn't right despite the atmosphere of cheer.

Before he could second-guess himself, Jeremy jumped onto the float and extended his hand to help Ruby up. Her simple "Thank you" reassured him she thought his behavior appropriate.

The marching bands hoisted their instruments and the parade was underway. As the floats proceeded slowly along Casper Lake Drive, Jeremy scanned the path. Plenty of space separated groups of spectators clustered on both sides of the street. To his right, beyond the people, Casper Lake stretched to the horizon. Open spaces, clean air and a celebration to bring the town together. Jeremy added his silent prayer of thanks to the other prayers certain to be offered today.

As the parade curled toward the business district, the crowds grew exponentially. At this speed, he estimated the procession would take another thirty minutes to round the corner and complete the run down Main Street. People peered and pointed as the marching bands and floats as they came into view. But there was one exception.

Amid the sea of faces, someone stood out with their back to the parade. Jeremy squinted at the strip of businesses along the main drag, but at over three hundred yards, he couldn't discern enough details to identify the person or determine which store had caught the person's attention.

Interested in Ruby's take, he tapped her arm, but when Jeremy looked again, the person had disappeared.

Ruby responded to his touch by looking over her shoulder. She smiled. "Fun, isn't it?"

A large bang interrupted the conversation, and the float ahead of them slowed. The tinkle of music faded as smoke trickled from underneath it and spewed up to form a cloud that hung like a portent of doom. Five minutes ticked by as its driver maneuvered the vehicle and trailer off the road.

"Oh no." Jeremy looked at Ruby, whose smile had morphed into a frown. She jumped down and hurried forward to speak with the driver, who gestured to the disabled engine, shrugged and shook his head.

The hair on the back of Jeremy's neck stood up. Did the fact that the float housed town commissioners earmark it for sabotage? Or was it a diversion to strand everyone, orchestrated by who-ever had been staring at the businesses instead of the parade?

He heard Ruby call his name, so he jumped off the float to join her and the rest of the group, which consisted of Tom Ewan, Grant Grud and the three other commissioners. Frank Dosser ar-rived from his post at the front, red-faced and out of breath from the effort. "What's going on?" he asked.

"This trailer's not going anywhere," the driver said.

Frank ran both hands over his head. "I don't be-lieve it. Breakdowns and delays are the worst pub-licity ever. Can't anybody do anything?" He poked his finger at Ruby. "You're the sheriff. Fix this."

Ruby smiled, though Jeremy could see some redness creep up her neck. His own neck muscles tightened, the result of holding his anger in check.

"Now just hang on there, Frank," Grant inter-ceded. "You may order your staff around, but when you address our esteemed sheriff, please show respect."

Frank rolled his eyes.

Commissioner Tom held up his hand for silence. "Before everyone goes ballistic, maybe the sher-iff should investigate. But I imagine if someone messed with the float's engine, they're aiming to humiliate us and not you, Mr. Mayor."

Grant rubbed his hands together. "Tom, you may be overly sensitive. And even if your point has validity, the sheriff's no more qualified to examine motor engines than me. Now, if Mr. Kell were around…"

"The retired coroner, what good would he be?" Jeremy asked.

"He's great with mechanical stuff, but I don't see him in the crowd." Commissioner Tom craned his neck left and right.

"We're running out of time. We can't keep everyone waiting, not on Thanksgiving Day. Can't someone think of a solution?" Frank's mouth turned down.

"I can." Ruby spoke with quiet authority. "I've got four deputies on bikes. Jeremy and I make six. We can't carry all the commissioners, but two of you could sit in the folding chairs on the inner detachable platform. The other two can join our walking contingency and grab a corner of the platform. We'll stash the bikes on another float and pick them up at the end of the run."

"Sounds like a plan," Grant said enthusiastically. "And the commissioners can spell each other by taking turns sitting and walking."

Ruby's plan did seem to cover the bases, but Jeremy hesitated. In one fell swoop, this parade glitch had made sure to divert everyone's attention away from the businesses on Main and funneled it to Casper Lake Drive. It occupied all the people responsible for the town's administration and redirected the energy of the entire police force. *Might as well declare open season on crime in Tinker.* He glanced over at the disabled float, more convinced than ever it was the handiwork of the serial burglar. He needed a bicycle.

"What's going on? What's wrong?" Ruby asked.

"I'm not sure anything's wrong, but I'm forging ahead to double-check the security of businesses at the end of the parade route."

Jeremy didn't wait for an answer. He donned a helmet, grabbed a bicycle and pushed off from the side of the float. He began to pedal. Halfway to the end of the large northwest curve, where Casper Lake Drive joined Main Street, Jeremy remembered how he'd marveled at the newest electric bike launched in New York cycle shops only to decide it represented a luxury he couldn't afford. How he longed for one now.

He ducked his head, hunched his shoulders and pedaled furiously, slowing only when he reached Cappy's, the first business on the north side of Main. The stores in the block, all closed for the parade, appeared secure, which made him wonder if his imagination was working overtime.

There, two blocks farther down, the shadow of a person ducked into a doorway. Jeremy got off his bike and moved stealthily to his left. As he crept closer to his target, the sound of someone calling his name stopped him cold.

SEVENTEEN

"Mr. Lawson, the visual of you sneaking down the street like a cat stalking a mouse could qualify you for an award. I still think you and the sheriff should consider joining Tinker's theater troupe." Harvey Klingshot had rounded a corner and planted himself behind Jeremy on the sidewalk.

He sounded like he was speaking through a megaphone. Any chance of catching someone breaking into one of the businesses had evaporated. Maybe that was the point. Or maybe Harvey was the shadow he'd seen.

When Jeremy had mapped out Tinker's business district, he'd seen a lane connecting the backs of the building in the business district, a lane invisible from the fronts of the stores. It would be simple for someone casing a shop to circle back and approach Jeremy from behind. Harvey's distinctive green hat was nowhere in sight, and without it he could fade into the woodwork.

"Mr. Klingshot, I doubt whether the sheriff and

I have the time to devote to acting at least in the foreseeable future, but thanks anyway." Jeremy cushioned his words with a chuckle.

"Speaking of the sheriff, where is she?"

"Back with the rest of the parade. I came ahead."

"Good for you, breaking away from the herd to check on security."

"And why aren't you with the crowd? I saw you earlier speaking to Stanley Kell."

"Oh, I moved on. Had some stuff to look into and then figured I may as well stay here to watch the parade's end run. Got the perfect spot." Harvey stamped his feet to illustrate his point.

"And here it comes." Jeremy pointed and Harvey turned as Frank Dosser in the Grand Marshal's chair rounded the corner and the parade began its final stretch. Amid whoops and hollers, Ruby and the deputies combined piloting the corners of the platform with waves to the crowd. That she had provided the spark for the solution of the broken-down trailer didn't surprise Jeremy. Her fresh approach to situations was one of her most endearing attributes.

He glanced over at Harvey, who stared down the street as if hypnotized. Did his errands include prowling around the stores and alleyways of Tinker's commercial district? The jewelry store at the corner would look like the cherry atop a sundae to any would-be burglar. But Harvey's personality didn't fit the profile of someone who could sneak anywhere.

When the commissioner's platform drew alongside him, Jeremy lifted his bike onto the trailer, then stepped forward to walk beside Ruby. While everyone disembarked, he took her aside to discuss his suspicions.

"I can't see it," she insisted. "Harvey lacks subtlety, and he's never struck me as methodical enough to construct a long-term plan with the amount of detail that has characterized the serial burglaries."

"He's methodical enough to learn lots of lines to garner him the lead in those theater shows."

"Memorizing isn't the same as having an ability to visualize how all the parts fit into a whole. He acts in plays, he doesn't write them."

Jeremy swallowed. Ruby's logic appealed, but he couldn't shake the shroud of trepidation that dogged his thoughts. Breathe deep and relax? Not likely.

"Come on." Ruby grabbed his elbow. "Time to put you in a booth."

Deputy Deborah's prediction that 5,500 photos would disappear in an hour seemed to be coming true. Initially, the people crowded around the front of the booth, but Lucille stepped in and organized them into two lines, one for each hand she said, and chaos changed to calm. If Lucille were thirty years younger, he'd earmark her as the burglar. With her ability to see the big picture, find solutions and persuade people to do her bidding, Jeremy thought her personality and aptitudes were a perfect fit for his profile. He sighed, then smiled as the good citizens of Tinker and the surrounding area continued to ask him for his headshot.

Beyond the sea of faces, Jeremy could see sidewalks filled with families window-shopping or simply enjoying the fun atmosphere. The pumpkin-head people who had so delighted Ruby earlier mixed with the crowd. It seemed to Jeremy they had multiplied. Where once there were two, now there were two dozen.

Most appeared from a costume store down the street and began to mingle, but two hit the sidewalk from behind his booth. Some handed out candy to the children; some offered directions or provided information about the town to guests in Tinker for the day. Several carried rolls of stickers printed with whimsical drawings of vegetables. They would hand them out so people could plaster the image of a smiling carrot or dancing potato onto their shirts.

Everyone and everything formed part of the unified picture he'd come to associate with Thanksgiving, except for the two orange traffic cones placed on the sidewalk in front of the jewelry store. Had he seen them there earlier? With Harvey's distractions, he couldn't be sure.

Pedestrians skirted onto the road to avoid them, but Jeremy wondered who had put them in place. He was certain employees of public works or the road maintenance crews weren't working on the holiday. And he didn't think any small shop owner would willingly obstruct the shop's entryway by planting an obstruction in front of their business.

He scanned the crowd, caught Deputy Deborah's attention and waved her over to the booth.

"Ready to admit I was right, you superhero you?" Deborah grinned.

"Never in my wildest dreams did I envision being swamped by all these women." Jeremy shook his head in disbelief. Then he pointed to the traffic cones. "What's going on with those?"

"I'll check it out and get back to you."

Jeremy continued to hand out the photos and shake hands. The picture pile grew smaller, and he tried to focus on the people who wanted to say hello. He responded politely to remarks suggesting he run in the next election, all the while watching Deborah and keeping an eye out for Ruby.

At last he saw her. The sun reflected off Ruby's beige cowboy hat, and for a few moments, Jeremy stared, mesmerized by her beauty. A baby's shriek startled him out of his reverie. He rubbed his eyes and looked again. Ruby stood with Deborah and a man he assumed was the owner of the jewelry store, between the traffic cones. And in that moment he knew the orange markers were another diversion.

Jeremy marveled at the intellect of his adversary. The disabled float motor bought the prowler time to case his target a final time. Soon the parade ended and the stores reopened. The cones drew the owner out of his jewelry store, which left it unattended for at least a few minutes. The two distractions added up to one heist, this time for something of real value— priceless gold and silver.

He handed the final headshot to a woman, then turned to the back and tried to open the door of the booth. It stuck. He lowered his shoulder and rammed it into the wood. Nothing budged. He tapped all over the wood interior. There was no give, no loose boards. The minutes ticked by. He turned and leaned out toward the people who still crowded the front of the booth.

"Ruby!" He tried to shout over the noise of the Thanksgiving fair. She didn't notice him. He waved, all the while calling out her name.

Then the audience took up the chant. They shouted, "Ruby, Ruby, Ruby," in unison.

She looked over to him. A confused expression clouded her face. He bellowed, "Out!" and motioned at the booth's counter. He saw her speak to Deborah, who trotted back toward him. In less than a minute, the door to his booth swung open.

"It was latched," she said as he pushed past her and rounded the corner.

He had to get Ruby to go inside the jewelry store and check its security.

Ruby noted the expression on Jeremy's face was a mix of worry and determination. Trusting his instincts, and hers, she focused solely on him.

The crowd of spectators parted as Jeremy snaked his way over to her. It was hard to hear him over all the noise, but she could see his mouth moving.

"Go back inside!"

She suddenly made sense of his shouts. Ruby quelled the urge to run toward him and turned back to the jewelry store door. She was too late.

The owner, alarmed by the earlier ruckus, had pushed past Ruby and dashed into his shop. He began to shout. "I've been robbed!"

Ruby's heart sank. What could be worse than a midday robbery in the height of the Thanksgiving celebration? A panel of the glass display case to her right had been removed and a two foot square hole now housed only empty ring boxes and necklace display stands. An Employees Only door stood ajar.

Jeremy's form blocked the store's entrance. Ruby ran down the hall, twisted the knob of the back door and stepped out into an alley. She raced to the corner in time to see three pumpkin heads stop at a crosswalk. One turned left, one right, and the third pushed straight ahead through the crowd that continued to mill around in excitement.

Ruby blinked, rubbed her eyes and blinked again. She recognized the pumpkin head who'd crossed the street and moved away at a brisk pace. It was the back of the serial burglar, burned into her brain that night over three weeks ago, receding in front of her.

This was her chance to vindicate herself and crack the case. "Jeremy," she called, then pointed. "That pumpkin head is our serial burglar."

They took off running. Ruby could see Pumpkin Head, who must have sensed danger behind him, race another block. He squeezed through a gap in the fencing erected to discourage trespassers and entered the Ekler Building, cordoned off after fire destroyed portions of its interior six months earlier. There was nothing left for her to do but follow the leader.

The stench of charred wood assaulted Ruby first. The few sunbeams that penetrated the crumbling roof didn't provide enough light for her to see much more than the outline of shapes, remnants of cabinets and cupboards, and piles of debris that had originally belonged to tables or chairs. Although it had been half a year, ash and dust still hung in the air, stirred by breezes that seeped through exterior cracks on windy days.

A partially destroyed staircase allowed limited

access to the second floor; one wall of a room remained standing. But for all the destruction, the scorched back wall of the building stood intact.

A movement startled Ruby. Pumpkin Head emerged from behind what had once been a cabinet and crept toward the staircase.

His head jerked to his right at the same moment a floorboard creaked. Pumpkin Head froze in midstep then bounded up the stairs; Jeremy ran after him. Ruby caught her breath as the stairs swayed, but both men continued to climb. In no time, both had made it safely to the top.

Ruby could see only one way out for the burglar. He would have to climb through a second-floor window at the back of the building, which meant her best chance of apprehending him would be to leave the burned business now and circle the perimeter.

But before she had time to enact her plan, Jeremy lunged for Pumpkin Head.

Ruby heard a resounding crash and a grunt, and saw Jeremy hanging from the ceiling, his legs pedaling back and forth. He'd crashed through the weakened floorboards. Only his grip stopped him from falling onto a patch of charred wood a story below. Both hands clawed at the splintered edges of the hole.

"Hang on, Jeremy!" she yelled.

Ruby clenched her jaw, tamped down her fear and clambered up the stairs using her hands and feet. They wobbled precariously. Her breath caught in her throat.

She could see Jeremy as he tried to lever himself out of the hole with his arm strength. But his effort splintered the wood on the edges, causing the hole to widen. His shoulders looked bunched, and his taut arms were stretched to the max.

A slow creak sent chills down her spine. The fire-weakened flooring around him sagged. It was only a matter of time before it gave way completely.

Her stomach roiled, and the incapacitating images that visited whenever she confronted heights exerted an unnerving power over her. She may as well have been glued to the spot. Then Ruby's eyes widened. Pumpkin Head had stopped, turned back and bent toward Jeremy, then extended his hand, as if to help him regain his footing. *He's going to save him.*

Ruby stood, swayed and lurched toward the men. But she couldn't trust the floor to hold her weight. Pumpkin Head jerked his head up when Ruby moved, and he backed away from Jeremy, fleeing to the adjoining room.

It's all up to me.

Ruby spotted a radiator attached to a wall. She took off her belt, crouched down and secured one end to it. Gripping the other end, she crawled as far as she could toward Jeremy without risking more of the floor caving in. If she attempted to just grab Jeremy's arm and hoist him up, they would both plummet to certain death. But if she held on to the belt with both hands and stretched her legs, Jeremy could grab her boot. If she pulled hard enough, he could wedge himself up and out of the hole to freedom. At least, that's what she was praying for.

With her belt tied tight above her head, she kicked her legs toward Jeremy. *Stay in the present*, she commanded as her thoughts tried to take her back to the stormy night in the car with her husband. Her muscles ached with tension.

Ruby almost cried aloud when Jeremy tugged on her boot. She gritted her teeth, bent her legs and tried to force herself into the wall, away from Jeremy. The floor sagged as Jeremy thrashed in an attempt to heave himself to safety. He swung his legs through the air and up. He wriggled and inched closer to her. At last, his soot-covered torso lay beside her.

"Thanks. Thought I was a goner."

Ruby grasped his hand in hers. "No problem."

She would have loved to stay beside Jeremy, but when she looked sideways, Ruby could see Pumpkin Head angled close to a burned-out window midway down the outside wall of the Ekler Building. He was going to escape the way Ruby predicted.

EIGHTEEN

Ruby's duty to ensure Jeremy's safety and her reluctance to leave him warred with her desire to pursue the burglar.

"You're sure you're okay?"

"I'm sure. Go."

Ruby resisted the urge to look back at him or down at the blackened struts and crossbeams beneath her and focused on the squared opening in the exterior wall. If Pumpkin Head could do it, so could she. Ever so slowly, she picked her way across the room. A draft coming in from outside did little to remove the acrid odor that clung in her nose and lined her throat, so when she reached the window, she ignored the air's cold temperature and took huge gulps.

Ruby could see Pumpkin Head running down the street, away from the crowds and toward parade floats now parked in the lot beside the old train station.

He won't get away this time.

A metal fire escape, its structure twisted from

the earlier fire, extended the length of the building. Ruby swung first one leg then the other through the window, landed and almost slipped on the slanted metal slats.

Instead of looking down, she stared at the wall and gingerly began to lower herself. Her emotions swelled up as she continued to descend, but with a supreme effort, she willed herself to stay in the present. Once she touched solid ground, she turned to see Jeremy posed in the window frame, then broke into a run in the direction of the parking lot.

No more than four minutes had passed. Still she pushed herself as if running a one-hundred-yard dash and charged after Pumpkin Head. She rounded a corner, but a bicycle swerved out of the parking lot exit and forced her to skid to a stop. Her stomach dropped. It was Pumpkin Head getting away.

The float that had housed the commissioners, the one where the deputies' bicycles were stored, the one Pumpkin Head had no doubt raided to get his wheels, sat in a parking space halfway down the left row of vehicles. Ruby raced over, disentangled a bike and took off after him.

The bicycle wheels bounced in and out of small potholes, but she retained enough control to whiz past Jeremy now standing in the entry to the lot and make the turn onto Casper Lake Drive. A fork in the road one-quarter of a mile south forced Ruby to choose a direction. Due west led to the farthest-flung subdivision in Tinker, but she doubted the burglar would be willing to travel through traffic and slow for stoplights. Why do that when he could continue on Casper Lake Drive, which curved around the body of water for six miles, unimpeded by any road markings until it intersected the less-traveled subsidiary?

Decision made, she pedaled furiously. If it were any other circumstance, Ruby would enjoy the cold wind against her face and the feeling of freedom created by moving down the open road beside the water. But she knew better than to relax.

Two miles in, Ruby almost turned back. Her burning legs and aching shoulders made her question the point of continuing. She'd never catch him. Pumpkin Head had too big a lead. Then she remembered a shortcut.

A stand of Gambel oak started a hundred feet from her current position and extended straight across the southeast portion of the lake. A quick mental calculation proved she would reach the end of the thicket before Pumpkin Head reached the loop of Casper Lake. There was no time to lose.

Branches clawed at her jacket. Ruby pushed forward, then dropped down to the edge of the water to avoid the thickest area of brush. She angled her bike along the pencil-thin path to follow the lake's course. Beyond the bank, white froth outlined boulders that poked through the water and skimmed across patches of ice as Casper Lake narrowed on its journey to the falls.

When she reached the end of undergrowth, she dismounted, leaned her bike against a tree and hunkered down on the shoreline to wait. She anticipated Pumpkin Head should round the last curve of Casper Lake Drive and be on top of her in three minutes, enough time to prepare an ambush.

Ruby reached in her pocket for something to stretch across the road and create a tripwire, but her fingers closed on air. She tugged at the low-growing branches of the Gambel oak, hoping to build an obstruction, but nothing budged.

There was always her gun. Ruby loathed violence but wondered if she could justify a failure to use her weapon in this situation, particularly when the consequence of keeping it sheathed in her holster meant the burglar would escape again. Jeremy was nowhere in sight, but she was not alone.

Help me, please, God. I need to serve and protect everyone.

Firing a disabling shot provided a possible solution to her dilemma. The odds of it hitting Pumpkin Head were low. She could lower them further by aiming for the road ahead of him. He would startle, topple off his bicycle, and she could arrest him. Ruby removed her gun from its holster, stepped onto the road, adopted her shooting stance and waited.

Ruby saw the flash of orange as Pumpkin Head

crested the hill. All of her muscles tensed. Protocol dictated that she should give a warning. And she did. But the bicycle kept moving. Ten seconds passed and she pulled the trigger.

The shot exploded into the nearby woods; dozens of leaves and debris rained down. The front tire jerked, causing the bicycle to career off the road. These three actions happened in a millisecond and created instant chaos.

Pumpkin Head hurtled off the bike, landing in the narrows where Casper Lake became Casper River. His arms and legs flailed as he crashed onto and then skidded along a layer of just-formed ice covering a portion of the water. He almost smashed into a group of rocks but stopped himself in time. If he remained still, Ruby could rescue him the way she'd rescued Jeremy, by stretching out to reach him. But before she could move a muscle, he made what in her estimation was a fatal mistake. He tried to stand up. The ice creaked then cracked. He roared as his lower body plunged into the rapids.

Ruby raced to the shoreline. The fingers section of Casper Lake, renowned for the strength of its currents running through the Casper River from the main body of water to the falls, ranked high on the difficulty scale devised by white-water-rapid enthusiasts. Signs warned prospective boaters of the dangers. But there was no time to think about that now.

Ruby hated getting cold and wet, but the water had swept Pumpkin Head off his feet, giving her no choice. Time to exercise the "protect" mandate of her oath. She didn't need extra weight, so tossed her jacket on the bank before jumping into the river. Her teeth chattered as she fractured the thin sheets of ice that separated them, but she drew closer, grabbed an arm and pulled hard.

Pumpkin Head immediately propelled himself toward Ruby. Closer to the shore, he dug his free leg into the riverbed and levered himself upright, grasped Ruby's shoulders and pushed down.

His behavior shocked her. Ruby yelped. As he submerged her, frigid water sloshed into her mouth and up her nose. She wrestled to the surface and gave Pumpkin Head a mighty push even while she coughed, choked and gasped for air. Pumpkin Head regained his footing, then turned away from her again.

"Don't," she croaked. "You'll never make it."

"Watch me," he said, and took a first giant step onto the shore. But the sight of Jeremy poised on the bank, backlit by the setting sun, froze Pumpkin Head midstride.

Ruby's eyes widened as she watched Jeremy jump straight up to grasp a branch of Gambel oak. Surely he couldn't be thinking of crossing the river that way. But before she could blink, he'd swung his legs back and forth, built up speed and then launched himself through the air.

When he plowed into the burglar, both men fell. Arms and legs flailing, they thrashed and rolled into the icy water. Their momentum combined with the river current pulled them closer the falls.

Ruby screamed. She too swam with the current but angled toward shore. Her legs kicked like pistons. Although the edge of the falls loomed, if she stretched to the max, Ruby could just reach a single overhanging branch of gamble oak where its tip touched the water. Every muscle hurt as she grabbed, heaved and crab-walked with her free arm and legs. She forced herself to ignore Pumpkin Head and Jeremy while she hauled herself up the bank and collapsed on the ground.

Cold and wet, she longed to close her eyes just for a second. But her sense of duty, her pride and adrenaline forced her onto her hands and knees. Ruby could see the men, now formed into a giant ball, perched on the brink of Casper Falls. She said a quick prayer for their safety.

Everyone local knew to stay away from the rapids. Treacherous water spelled danger. Jeremy's unfamiliarity with the area, desire to arrest Pumpkin Head, and maybe even anger at the man who'd tried to hurt her could explain his behavior. But everything she knew about the burglar suggested he was local, which meant his bravado outweighed his common sense. Or maybe Pumpkin Head believed he was indestructible. Either way, it would be up to Ruby to pick up the pieces.

By the time she scrambled down the incline, both men had disappeared. Farther along, she spotted Pumpkin Head, underneath Jeremy at the moment, his head lolled back and lodged partially underwater.

Jeremy stood upright but staggered sideways. A gash over his left eye oozed blood, and she could see numerous small cuts on his hands and arms.

There wasn't a moment to lose. Ruby waded into the slower, safer part of the river, grabbed Pumpkin Head under the armpits and pulled him upright to a sitting position. She braced his back with her leg. He sputtered. His limbs flopped. He tried but couldn't muster enough coordination to stand.

Jeremy came up to the pair.

"Let's see who we've got here." He reached out and removed the burglar's orange headgear.

Ruby gasped. "Stanley Kell. I don't believe it."

A minute ticked by before Stanley spoke. "Nothing personal. I got bored, is all."

"Nothing personal? You got bored? That's okay, then?" Ruby glowered, her hands balled into tight fists.

"I resent your sarcastic tone. Forced retirement didn't come easy. When the commissioners turned down my request for an exception to the three-term rule, they thought I was past it. Me. Past. It."

"So, you became a burglar? Terrorizing your friends and neighbors?"

"I just wanted to try it once, prove I could sneak in and out of a place. But once wasn't enough. It's all about the adrenaline rush."

"Don't you get an adrenaline rush playing squash or competing in triathlons?"

"Sure." Stanley shrugged, "But the rush I got breaking into places was bigger."

"What about a plan that included running for coroner again in the upcoming election?"

"Oh, I planned to run. And I'd win. And the crimes would stop. You can't have a coroner spending his spare time being a burglar."

"I still don't understand. You knew as sheriff, I'd have to investigate."

Stanley's mouth turned down, then he pointed an accusing finger at Ruby. "I didn't expect you to solve it. You could've investigated but avoided chasing me and tracking me down. Handled the burglaries the way you've been handling the murder you consulted me about."

"So when someone reports a prowler, I'm supposed to let it slide?"

"You ramped things up and endangered people. Look at me now. Cold and sopping wet with all these cuts and scrapes. You're lucky I didn't break any bones."

"I'm to blame for your reckless behavior?"

Stanley didn't reply and instead turned to Jeremy. "You contributed to this mess too. Your irresponsible actions could've got us killed. Who in their right mind jumps on another person in the middle of a river in November?"

"You brought that on yourself, partner," Jeremy said. "I saw you wrestling with Ruby. Mess with her, you deal with me."

Stanley's face grew red. "You think you're up for it? I'm an Ironman with the medals to prove it. You're a *consultant* who's graduated from a desk in the big city to a puppy-dog post in a small town. I doubt you've spent more than ten minutes in a gym. And I've navigated over those falls numerous times without a scratch. Without you on my back, I'd have made it this time too."

"Enough. The longer we stand here jawing, the colder we'll be. Let's take this to the station. Turn around Stanley." Ruby cuffed him, then they climbed back up the incline to the car.

NINETEEN

Ruby stood by her office window, staring. Jeremy placed his hand on her shoulder.

"I doubt you're admiring the setting sun," he said.

She spoke, her voice just above a whisper. "I feel awful. Arrest made, beautiful evening, a community Thanksgiving dinner dance to begin at six, and I can't shake this nagging disappointment."

"You closed the case."

"No, we closed it. Stanley's statement pretty much confirmed what you'd already deduced. A perp you described as an intelligent, organized thrill seeker who ramped up the stakes is behind bars. But the fact is the accused happens to be a colleague I respected."

"I get the impression Stanley was a close friend."

"He was. He supported me after my husband passed. Said the right things, helped me work through my grief. I owed him. How did I express my gratitude? I hunted him down and threw him in jail."

"You can't blame yourself for doing your job. You didn't know the identity of who you were pursuing. Still angry at him?"

"Not so much. I thought he betrayed me, but now I get it wasn't personal."

"He's suffering from an addiction."

"Somehow that doesn't make me feel a whole lot better."

Jeremy wished he could take Ruby in his arms and make everything bad go away. He felt so connected to this woman. Her pain was his pain. Yet he feared she might misinterpret his overtures.

She hadn't reacted when he'd told Stanley if he messed with Ruby, he'd have to deal with him. When he'd blurted out the adage, Jeremy mentally kicked himself. Caught in the heat of the moment, angered that someone, anyone, would try to hurt Ruby, he'd given in to the impulse to declare his intention to shield her from threats and defend her by any means necessary.

But he refused to take advantage of her vulnerable state. He wanted her to want him, not because of a feeling of duress or out of a sense of obligation but because it was a positive choice made by an independent woman.

He continued to stand with a calming hand on her shoulder.

Ruby turned to Jeremy and looked up at him. Her raw, natural beauty astonished him. Caught in a beam from the sunset, her lips shone, soft and inviting. The light glanced off her upturned face. Before he could second-guess himself, Jeremy bowed his head and pressed his lips against hers. He'd never felt more complete.

When they broke apart, Ruby's brows furrowed. "That was nice," she said. "Very nice. But I'm not sure we should open that door."

"You mean so much to me. Only a month and you're on my mind every waking moment."

"I think of you often too. But there are complications."

"Complications?"

"Yes. I wonder how stamping Case Closed on the serial burglary matter impacts your future? You were brought here to help solve it. Is it time to go back to New York?"

"I don't know. Do you want me to stay?"

"I'm not sure my opinion matters."

"It matters to me."

Ruby frowned. "I have feelings for you, but I'm also afraid. Asking me whether you should stay here in your capacity as a crime analyst is a lot for me to process right now. It's like adding spaghetti and meatballs on top of my plate of fish-and-chips, handing me a fork and expecting me to polish everything off."

"Sorry."

"Don't apologize. The truth is I'm not sure. I do know I wasn't consulted when the commissioners hired you, and not being privy to the details of your employment agreement, I have no idea whether your transfer hinged on the conclusion of an event or on time."

Jeremy pulled his phone out of his pocket. "Maybe I'd better find out."

He stepped away from Ruby and pressed speed dial. The connection crackled so much he began to wonder if New York was in the midst of a rare November snowstorm, but eventually his old supervisor came on the line.

"Jeremy, I hear you're a star. Congratulations. Big city meets small town. Guess you showed them some new tricks. You cracked that serial burglary case in record time, under a month."

"Thank you, sir."

"And things over here couldn't be better. Everything's gone according to plan. Just last week the media rated us among the top crime-busting agencies across the state. Everyone's still aware of you, but in a good way."

"Nice to hear," Jeremy said.

"So, when are you coming back?"

"Sir?"

"To New York. You didn't think we'd hang you out to dry in no-man's-land, did you?"

"Have you talked to Commissioner Ewan?"

"Tom? Sure. Today. We hadn't spoken since the night before you left for Tinker, but he was so happy you solved the case, he called right away and told me what happened."

"Did you discuss me going back there?"

"Not specifically. But I assumed you'd be champing at the bit. We can feed the media news about your latest success and point out how we're in the process of rectifying the negative associated with your absence. You've played ball on this thing, so get in line for a new office and a hefty salary increase. It's a win-win."

How often in the past month had Jeremy heard that phrase? He'd come to associate it with trouble, having found his best interests didn't usually figure into the equation.

"I'm not sure."

"How can that be?"

"Well, I'm still involved here. There are other crimes I'm working on, a murder for instance."

"Other crimes? A murder? Sounds like they're taking advantage of your expertise. You know that here we like to parcel the work out so no one gets overloaded. Wrap up one case, then move on to the next."

"Actually, I'm enjoying the multitasking."

"Well good for you, but I'm surprised. Always took you for a city slicker. Figured the pace of a small town might not gel so well."

"It's gelled fine, sir."

"If I didn't know better, I'd think you don't want to come back to New York. You could stay in Tinker, of course, but you realize you're committing to a lower salary with less room for advancement.

And I'd have no further input in your employment situation."

"Which makes Commissioner Tom Ewan my supervisor, correct?"

"Technically, no. I spoke to Tom originally because he's my friend, but my understanding is all the commissioners agreed to your transfer. If New York steps away, the corporate body is responsible for your appointment and salary. The local sheriff is your direct boss. But you know all this. I'm sure Tom explained it to you when you arrived."

No, Tom didn't.

"Can I get back to you about staying here?"

"Sure, Jeremy, sure. I can give you a week. But for the record, if I'd known you'd be thinking about staying on in Tinker, I might not have sent you there in the first place. We need you here."

Jeremy said goodbye and clicked off, worried. Ruby had referred to her full plate, but now his overflowed too.

Commissioner Tom fibbed. Jeremy kicked himself; he should have known. Straight shooters discussed. Commissioner Tom preferred manipulation tactics: misstatements, exaggerations, even veiled threats.

Assuming his reelection, Commissioner Tom would remain in the picture. How much time did Jeremy want to spend politicking around this impediment? Buttering up people in power had never been his strong suit.

There was the question of the murder. Jeremy's scientific knowledge, helpful to discern patterns in the burglaries, was not as relevant when applied to the homicide investigation. He and Ruby were on the verge of its solution, he could feel it in his bones. But it would be solved using logic and old-fashioned detective work. Ruby's way. She didn't need him here, but he still wanted to be present when they slapped the cuffs on the killer.

And what of his job once they solved the murder? The other deputies had referred to Tinker as quiet and had said the current spate of crimes was unusual. Did Tinker need another deputy? Would he be hired full-time in that capacity? Or maybe he could be tasked with being the crime analyst for the larger county. Worst-case scenario, there was always the possibility of making the longer commute to Denver.

But Ruby was his biggest reason to carve out a life in Tinker. He'd never felt such a strong bond with a woman. The attraction was magnetic. He couldn't imagine his life without her in it. But he knew she still had doubts. About him? Herself? He needed to convince her of his intentions if he were to fulfill his dream and stay in Tinker.

"What's the word from New York?" Ruby raised her eyebrows and tipped her head.

"They want me back." Was it his imagination or did her expression darken for a moment.

"And?"

"They gave me a week to decide."

"So, there's talk of you remaining in Tinker?"

"I'm not sure."

I'm not sure. That meant New York was calling his name. Could she or Tinker compete?

When he'd asked her how she felt about the possibility of his staying in Tinker, she didn't have an immediate answer. Why couldn't her head follow her heart?

Her heart said, *Yes, yes, yes.*

Jeremy was the first man since her husband passed who caught and kept her attention when he made a helpful suggestion, when his arm brushed hers, when he looked across the room and raised his eyebrows with his mouth slightly open in mock surprise at a comment she made. A man who focused and listened whether she spoke about the minutiae of a baseball game or a nuance of a case. A man prepared to take a dunking and ride the falls to ensure her safety. And that kiss.

Her head said, *Don't trust your heart.*

Your heart blinds you, she told herself. It makes you act like a schoolgirl with a crush on the football hero when you may be reacting out of loneliness to a fella foisted on you by circumstance. A fella who walks into the picture and, after getting what he wants, ducks out again to ride off to greener pastures. She didn't think that description fit Jeremy. But could she trust that judgment?

In fact, her plate was full simply caring for herself. Better not to complicate her life by allowing anyone else to get close. She should push Jeremy away and encourage him to return to New York. That was the rational course of action.

Ruby sighed. She had mulled over her options without reaching a firm conclusion. Her heart and head would still war, at least for a while.

She was tired and dirty and still partly wet from the encounter at Casper River, but her duties as sheriff hadn't ended yet. Not on this night. Tinker's annual Thanksgiving dinner and dance was scheduled to begin in less than two hours and she had an obligation to attend.

She'd gone solo the last four years, but at least now her head and her heart agreed. This year people would see her escorted by the man from New York, and it was what she wanted.

Ruby smiled sadly. This event might be their last social appearance before he left town for good.

TWENTY

The smell of roasted turkey filled the large room. Green bean casseroles and bowls of mashed potatoes and bread stuffing filled the tables, along with platters of meat, gravy boats and dishes of cranberries. Wreaths made from yellow, red and green leaves hung from the beamed ceiling. Scarecrows standing in the corners of the room contributed to the rustic atmosphere and signified a Thanksgiving celebration was afoot.

The setting reminded Jeremy of the opening scene from a play he'd enjoyed in New York. The critics had labeled it quaint. Here, "quaint" replaced the grays and blues of banquet rooms and clean lines of metal furniture. "Quaint" spoke to a different lifestyle, one Jeremy had grown to love.

Everyone wore a happy face and had a kind word for their neighbor. Well, almost everyone. Jeremy could see Anna Jones, flanked by Harvey and Lucille, standing motionless in front of a chair frowning.

"She has to be one of the unhappiest people in

Tinker," Ruby said. "I don't think I've ever seen her smile."

Jeremy nodded his agreement, then leaned over to ask a waitperson if the seating had been predetermined. When he learned it was not, he and Ruby headed toward the group of three.

"Follow my lead, okay?" he said. "Ladies, Harvey. Mind if we join you?"

Anna glared, Lucille gushed and Harvey slapped Jeremy on the back.

"You gals look lovely tonight," he said. "Anna, your necklace sets off your outfit. Lucille, those earrings highlight your eyes."

Lucille blushed. "Thank you. I love jewelry. Heirloom rings, earrings, necklaces and bracelets make up half of my collection, but I still enjoy shopping locally for baubles that catch my eye."

As other guests began to take their seats, Anna excused herself to go to the washroom. After she'd left the table, Lucille shielded her mouth with her hand and said, "You're wasting your breath giving her compliments. Anna's stuff, that's a different story. Her pieces are usually knockoffs."

"I wouldn't know how to tell a knockoff from the real thing," Ruby said.

"Oh, there are ways. The luster of a gem or the feel of the metal can differ, and replicas rarely have watermarks."

"You know quite a bit about the subject," Jeremy said.

"Jewelry's always been a passion of mine, even growing up."

"I hear congratulations are in order," Harvey interrupted. "You folks made an arrest."

"We did," Ruby confirmed. "I'm happy to say the case of the serial burglar has been put to bed. We caught him red-handed and got a full confession."

Anna, who had returned to the table in time to hear Harvey's comment and Ruby's reply, pursed her lips. "You still haven't solved the mystery of the bones, you know, the murder you use as an excuse to poke into people's business."

"We haven't," Ruby agreed.

"But we will, and soon," Jeremy said.

"Attention." The mayor rose from his seat on the elevated platform and walked over to a podium. "I want to officially welcome everyone to our community shindig. It's been another stellar year, and I say that both as a proud member and one of the leaders of this great Tinker community. Let's toast the season."

Ruby picked up her glass of white grape juice and took a sip, but she'd barely set it back on the table when the mayor turned and addressed the people seated alongside him. "And now let me introduce one of our esteemed commissioners, Tom Ewan."

Amid applause, the commissioner stood and took the microphone from the mayor. "I have good news," he proclaimed. "I'm happy to report the criminal who victimized our community for the last six months is in jail. The serial burglar's reign of terror has ended. Let's give a special thanks to Jeremy Lawson, the crime analyst I imported to assist the sheriff. Take a bow, sir."

Jeremy felt heat creep up his neck. He disliked being singled out as a hero, particularly when, in his opinion, Ruby had done far more. He looked at her, but she moved her head toward the ceiling, indicating he should stand. Jeremy rose and bowed. The applause intensified. People began to rise.

"An ovation for Tinker's newest star. Let's go, Jeremy," the commissioner started to chant.

As the crowd joined in, Jeremy held out his arms for calm. "No one acts alone," he said. "I'd like to share the spotlight with the person who led the crime-fighting team, Sheriff Ruby Prescott."

When her name was announced, Ruby stood, waved and immediately sat down again.

"And now," the commissioner said, "it's my pleasure to introduce Pastor Emeritus Henry Miller to lead us in prayer."

"Lord, we gather today to give thanks to for this bountiful feast. We are blessed to drink from Your waters and gain sustenance from Your lands, to live in harmony as we listen to Your Word and strive to do Your bidding each day. Grant us prosperity and peace. Amen."

Jeremy waited a moment before picking up his

knife and fork. He surveyed the room. The sight of folks passing heaping platters of turkey and scooping mashed potatoes onto their plates reminded him: the power of food lay as much in its ability to unite as in its ability to provide energy. They might need him in New York, but it felt good to be in Tinker.

The meal tasted as scrumptious as it smelled, but Jeremy restrained himself and declined a second helping. Sated, he sat back and resisted the urge to rub his stomach. If he never moved again, he'd be happy.

"May I have this dance?" Lucille's eyes shone.

"I'm honored." Jeremy escorted her to the center of the dance floor, a section of the room which had been cleared for this purpose. He began to move his feet in a box step to the three-quarter time of the waltz music.

While he guided Lucille around the floor, Jeremy looked for Ruby. He finally saw her moving from table to table, shaking hands and speaking with people, often sitting in an empty seat beside someone when talking for any length of time. She looked as natural in this setting as she did when performing her sheriff's duties.

He noticed Lucille had relaxed and shut her eyes while they danced. When the song ended, she asked, "Another?"

"Certainly."

The next tune, a rock and roll selection, stymied

him, so he waited to see how Lucille wanted to move. She still kept their connection by holding his hands but began to sidestep. "I'm doing the mashed potato," she said. "It was a big favorite in the sixties. Just follow me."

Jeremy looked down at her feet and tried to concentrate but began to stumble and misstep within a minute. He and Lucille started to laugh. "Guess I'm not cut out for this. I feel like I'm an octopus juggling eight legs. We'd better sit down before I trip you."

By the time Jeremy and Lucille returned to their seats, a crowd of older women gathered, each eager for a spin with him on the dance floor. He decided escorting the women in two-steps and foxtrots could be equated to Ruby working the room, a necessary activity for any public figure.

Finally Jeremy had a chance to sit and rest. Ten minutes later, Ruby rejoined him.

"Busy night." She grinned.

"Oh yeah. Everyone wants a twirl around the dance floor, but after our day today, I don't know how much longer I can hold up."

"Agree, but acknowledging people is an important part of the job, almost as important as arresting bad guys. Tell you what, let's sit here and enjoy the atmosphere for a while. But before we leave, I'd like to take a twirl myself."

"It'll be my pleasure."

* * *

Ruby smiled to herself. It was hard to imagine a more perfect evening. Good food, good people, tolerably short speeches. Nights like this reminded her of the reason she remained in Tinker. Though others had been quick to follow opportunities in the larger cities, and everyone would have understood if she'd left the small town behind after the accident took her husband's life, Ruby did not regret her choice to stay.

As she and Jeremy moved across the dance floor, she tuned out everyone else to focus on him. The scent of his aftershave—a warm woodsy aroma—drew her closer. Sheltered in his arms, a sense of safety enveloped Ruby. It had been so long since she'd felt this way toward any man. Too long.

She laid her head against him, shut her eyes and concentrated on the rhythm of his chest as it rose and fell. If only the sensation she was floating on a cloud could last forever. They danced to one song after another.

At first, Ruby let her mind wander, but the longer they danced, the more she began to wonder if taking the next step in a romantic relationship was a good idea.

He's always putting me ahead of himself.

After a day of sprinting down roads, wrestling in a burned-out building and bicycling to the Casper Rapids only to take a dunking and go over the falls, Jeremy had to be exhausted. Yet he seemed comfortable as they continued to dance the night away.

Initially, she'd tamped down irritation when she interacted with the new guy from New York. But over the past weeks, she'd come to understand an assumed arrogance was really a confidence in technology and himself. Both deserved.

Jeremy cared about the people around him. He held his nephew in high esteem and talked of regular video calls with his relatives in New York. Weekends spent hiking the trails around Tinker dovetailed with her penchant to build a photo gallery of candid nature shots by walking through Rock Garden Park and the forested areas of Tinker. Yes, they did have a lot in common.

And Jeremy had made his feelings about a deepening relationship clear when they'd relaxed in front of the Kissing Camels.

Nope, she was the biggest impediment to taking their relationship to the next level.

She'd been afraid to show weakness, fearful Jeremy would somehow take her vulnerability, turn it around and use it against her. But he'd been a source of comfort during her meltdown at the squash court when her fear of heights overpowered her.

Was she still too much in love with her late husband to entertain similar emotions with another man? Two years ago, the answer would be yes;

today Ruby was no longer certain. She still cherished every moment she'd spent with Adam, but Ruby had come to understand she could continue to love him; he'd always be in her heart. And she couldn't believe God's plan for her would include a life spent alone, never to respond to a man's caring and compassionate ways again.

But was this man the right one? Someone who still wasn't sure they could commit to building a relationship and a life in Tinker, far from the madding crowd. If she took herself out of the mix, what did Tinker hold for Jeremy?

"Hey, what's with the pensive look? Dancing is supposed to be fun."

"I'm having fun, but I was also thinking about the attractions of Tinker compared with a bigger city."

"And your conclusion?"

"I'm not sure the town can measure up."

"I disagree. Speaking as a newcomer, you can't discount the attraction of the wilderness. There are job opportunities, and if they don't happen, Denver is within commuting distance. And the biggest attraction of all from my point of view is you, Ruby Prescott."

She hadn't been in the market for romance when she met him, but after five years alone, maybe it was time to take a second chance at love, to relinquish the need to protect others from the nicks and scratches life would invariably throw their way, and to deepen her relationship with Jeremy.

Too soon, the music ended.

Jeremy bowed, then kissed her hand. "Thank you for the dance," he said.

"I've loved every minute."

As Ruby walked over to get her coat, she wondered if she could ever feel as special as she had this evening with Jeremy.

TWENTY-ONE

The air was chilly. Overnight precipitation had deposited a light dusting of snow on tree branches and car windshields. Traffic had been light. There were still a few hours before Black Friday kicked into full gear, which in Tinker was as likely to include reduced prices for recreational activities as store sales.

Five a.m. and all was quiet at the office too. No one Jeremy would have to talk to, no ringing phones. Now was the time to catch up with paperwork.

He headed to his desk and booted up the computer. As he settled in, he clicked through his emails. He read one, a reply sent to him by a major distributor of custom jewelry.

Sorry, our sales records only go back ten years.

So that was it. Every other distributor had already nixed the possibility of obtaining records. With this latest confirmation, there'd be no way to identify the purchaser of jewelry over fifty years ago.

Jeremy was reluctant to give up. There must be another way to track down the owner of the earring left in the trunk with the skeleton. He rested his chin on his hand but looked up when Ruby arrived.

"Good morning," she greeted him and waved a paper she held in her hand. "I've got something better than a deep discount sale price—I've got the report of the handwriting analyst. He confirmed Lucille probably signed the Crispin receipt."

"Probably?" Jeremy opened his mouth and widened his eyes in mock surprise. "I know there's a false positive rate of 3.1 percent, and that people have alleged handwriting analysis is a pseudoscience, but it has been admitted in some courts."

"And it should be enough to get me a search warrant for Lucille's home. What else we got?"

Ruby pulled over the whiteboard. Jeremy spread photos of the victim, suspects, the interior of the trunk and the prop room on the table. He stacked Lucille's bird journals at one end and placed maps of the theater and the homes of Lucille and Anna at the other. Ruby left the room and returned with the earring sent back by the anthropologist, the copy of the receipt for the gravestone bought to mark the resting place of Eleanor and the report of the handwriting analyst.

"We'll have to confront Lucille with all this. I'll lead off the discussion by saying everything points to her having murdered Eleanor." Jeremy crossed his arms.

"Despite the fact Harvey described Lucille as having no personality and all the witness statements refer to her as Eleanor's best friend?"

"Yep." Jeremy nodded.

"I'll pretend I'm a judge considering granting a search warrant. Convince me."

Jeremy tipped his imaginary cowboy hat. "Yes, ma'am." He stepped forward and began making his case. "Eleanor's bones were found in the old Grand Theater, one hundred yards away from Lucille's primary residence, a residence which is modest compared to what a woman of her means could afford. A woman, I might add, who by all accounts enjoys flaunting her wealth. Don't forget Lucille's parents owned lots of property, which would have given her a selection of less isolated homes to choose as her primary residence. But she's lived in that foursquare for over fifty years."

"True."

"People tend to choose homes for practical reasons. They may have little kids and want to be close to a school, or they may want to be able to access public transportation. Lucille's home is isolated, accessible only by a single road. The only thing in the area is a defunct theater, which we discovered was home to a skeleton. But that place is within eyeshot of her house, particularly if she uses binoculars."

"Which she does. So, you think she's lived there because she needed to keep an eye on the body, make sure no one else found out about it?" Ruby raised her eyebrows.

"Exactly. If we look at Anna's home, it's nowhere near the theater."

"Okay." Ruby nodded her head slowly. "But why report the prowler? Lucille's call and my response ultimately led to the skeleton being discovered."

"Look at it from her point of view. Lucille sees evidence of someone inside the theater and becomes frightened they'll find the skeleton if they spend too long poking around. She calls the sheriff, hoping a deputy will scare the prowler out of the theater before anyone discovers anything. It just didn't work out that way."

"All right."

"Eleanor disappears and the theater doors close. The venue's never refurbished or torn down. In fact Lucille claimed she couldn't bear to go back inside because of the memories. But she didn't want it to fall apart, not if it's harboring a skeleton. So she hired a maintenance man to take care of the place."

"Wouldn't she be worried he'd discover the body?"

"I don't think so. As his boss, she would give

him instructions on where to go and what to do. She could tell him to leave the backstage area alone or not to move anything in the prop room."

"We can get a statement from him attesting to the terms of his employment." Ruby made a note.

"And in spite of any aversion to the place, Lucille was quick to violate your crime scene, likely to check on the status of the skeleton."

"This is all interesting, but it doesn't prove guilt."

"There's more. Her alibi can't be confirmed. She places herself at the theater with Eleanor, but the only two people who can corroborate her story are dead."

"So you say we've got a woman without an alibi who acts suspiciously after her best friend disappears. Anything else?"

"Lots. The crime scene photos show the open trunk, the boxes stacked on shelves, the other props for *Costume Party*. If you look closely, you can see the decades-old Pixy Stix wrappers on the floor shoved half under a bottom shelf, which Lucille referred to in her original statement. Insider knowledge. They put her with Eleanor in the room."

"Go on."

"What we don't have are scripts. No scripts anywhere. Remember, according to Harvey, a script is essential to an actor until the curtain goes up. Now if Lucille had returned to the theater after speaking with Billy and found Eleanor gone, she would have taken her own script. I get it. But where's the other one?"

"Eleanor took it with her."

"But Eleanor never left the theater. We know that now."

"Right. So maybe Lucille took it."

"Maybe she did, and possibly kept it. Given all of the reasons I've just listed, plus a receipt with a forged signature, I think you should get a search warrant."

"I agree."

Jeremy grinned. He loved closing in on a murderer, even if it meant arresting the woman who had been the first to welcome him to Tinker.

Ruby picked up the earring from the table and held it aloft. "I think this case might hinge on the jewelry. The forensic anthropologist had it appraised. This is pricey."

"So?"

"So, for sure she keeps the other. No woman throws away one expensive earring of a pair in case its mate shows up later in a nook or cranny. Over the years she searches for it in her home, on the grounds, at the theater. She either doesn't think of or doesn't want to open the trunk with Eleanor inside to see if it's there."

"I can visualize it."

"So can I." Ruby shuddered. "Bad enough when I stumbled on those bones, but to voluntarily open the trunk knowing what's inside, I think you'd have to be made of stone."

Jeremy got a box and began to put their evidence inside. "While I clean up, you go get that search warrant. Then we can pay Lucille a visit."

The visit started off on a pleasant note.

Jeremy, Ruby and Lucille sat at her kitchen table, sipped tea, ate cookies and looked at pictures from old yearbooks. Lucille pointed out class photos and shots of club members. In some of the larger pictures, pinpointing Lucille was difficult, but as she flipped through the pages to the theater group or chess club, she appeared front and center. Even in candid shots, her grooming was impeccable.

Invariably decked out in a necklace, Jeremy couldn't tell if it was an authentic piece or costume jewelry.

"You wear a lot of bling," Jeremy said.

"Bling," Lucille repeated. "That's what they call it now. Well, I've always thought a necklace and earrings complete an outfit."

"Any style you favor?"

"I used to have a lot of fancy jewelry, but I gave some bits away and lost others over the years. Most of the stuff in these pictures was costume, but for special events, my mother allowed me to wear some eye-catching original pieces."

"Anything like this one?" Ruby produced the earring, a pink sapphire encased in gold.

Lucille gasped, then reached for it. "Beautiful." She turned the earring over in her fingers, cradling it as tears filled her eyes.

"It's yours, isn't it?" Jeremy asked.

"Where did you find it?"

"At the Grand Theater, in the trunk with the skeleton."

"I should have known. Eleanor was always taking things, had a bit of a problem that way. She must have pocketed it at one of our visits to my house."

"You're not denying it's yours then?" Ruby held out her hand and Lucille placed the earring in her palm.

"Oh, it's mine. I thought I lost it. I guess she took it with her, had it when she died. I thought she left for Hollywood, when all this time she and it were in that wretched theater. Can I keep it?"

"Sorry, it's evidence in a murder case." Ruby pushed the earring to one side. "In fact, I'd like to locate its mate, which you say you've got."

"Yes, upstairs in the jewelry box in my bedroom."

As Lucille pushed back her chair, Ruby pulled the search warrant out of her pocket and spread it on the table. "Please sit down. This piece of paper authorizes me to search for the earring and for anything else that might pertain to the homicide of Eleanor Costell."

Lucille plunked back into the chair, eyes wide, mouth open. "You suspect *me*? How ridiculous."

"Is it? Why have you stayed in this house when the only other building around was an abandoned theater you claimed to abhor?" Jeremy asked.

"I've stayed here because it's my home. I took my first step in this kitchen, said grace with my parents at this table. How could I leave?" Tears formed in her eyes.

"There've been other inconsistencies," Jeremy said. "You told us you couldn't bear to go into the theater after Eleanor left, but you went into it the first day we arrived to investigate."

"I had to see if there'd been any damage to my property—"

"No." Ruby's stern voice silenced Lucille's explanation. "I think you wanted to see if the skeleton had been discovered, and when you found the open trunk, took the opportunity to booby-trap the theater by putting soap on the floor."

Lucille shook her head. "It's not true. You're making a mistake."

"There's more," Ruby confirmed. "We interviewed people, tracked down clues."

Lucille scoffed. "People don't really know, memories are faulty. Things can often be misleading."

"Part of this search warrant authorizes me to

look for and take possession of any scripts of *Costume Party*. Harvey Klingshot told us actors personalize their scripts by writing in director's cues or highlighting scenes involving them. If I find two scripts here, I'm sure a handwriting analyst will be able to confirm if one of them belonged to Eleanor." Ruby crossed her arms and stared at Lucille.

Lucille still looked at them innocently, but slowly a wicked smile emerged. A shiver ran down Ruby's spine.

"It was Eleanor's fault, the fool. Up and leaving the way she said she was going to. Leaving me! When we'd promised each other we'd stick together, see things through. But Eleanor didn't understand loyalty…or friendship."

"Things got physical?" Jeremy asked.

Lucille stared through him, trapped in the memory.

"I begged her to stay and she laughed at me. I had become nothing more than a joke to her. We quarreled. She pushed past me, so I gave her a shove. Served her right. But I didn't mean for her to die! I've been filled with regret ever since."

"Why didn't you tell anyone?" Ruby could guess.

"Who would believe a sixteen-year-old? I panicked, put Eleanor in a trunk and did my best to forget."

"But you couldn't, could you?" Jeremy now held both Lucille's hands.

"Never," she whispered. "I'm eighty-one years

old, and I've been in jail every day since I decided to hide Eleanor and invent a story about Hollywood instead of calling the authorities."

"Do you feel better, getting this off your chest?" Jeremy asked.

"Not much. It's been years, decades, since I've felt good. I knew you were coming sooner or later and thought about jumping in my car and taking off. Can you imagine? An old lady, hands gripping the steering wheel, teeth bared, holding in a wordless scream."

"Not a pretty picture." Jeremy shook his head.

"No. Problem was, I've got nowhere to go." She sat back and folded her hands in her lap. Sweet as pie. "If you go into the study, you'll find Eleanor's script. I couldn't bear to part with it. I'd hidden her body, but I needed to keep a part of her closer to me than that trunk in the theater." Her chin raised, she said, "You know, I always was the better friend." Lucille stopped talking then, and a single tear rolled down her cheek. "You're going to arrest me, aren't you?"

Ruby nodded. "I'm sorry."

"Then can I please go upstairs and get my things?"

"Sure." Ruby helped Lucille out of her chair. "We'll wait down here."

Soon, Ruby heard shuffling overhead. She and Jeremy exchanged a sad glance.

Lucille came down the steps slowly, arms

loaded with two cardigans, a bath robe and several pill bottles.

"Let me help." Jeremy came forward and took the bottles.

"Thank you." Lucille moved toward the side door but stopped to face Ruby and Jeremy. "I was sorry about Eleanor and I'm sorry about this." She dropped the other items and revealed a gun. "I'll shoot if I have to. I just need time to get away."

Ruby's heart pounded and she heard a roaring in her ears. She could sense Jeremy measuring the distance between himself, Lucille and the door. She had already done the same.

Lucille inched closer to the door, propped it open and stood with one foot on the porch.

She's going to shoot him. Dear Lord, please, no. I can't let that happen.

Ruby lunged toward Lucille. The older woman's finger curled around the trigger, and she pulled it. Ruby shut her eyes, expecting to hear a bang and feel a burning pain in her chest, but nothing happened.

She opened her eyes, saw the gun lying on the floor, and stooped to pick it up. A theater prop. Lucille had bluffed them to make good her escape. But it didn't work. Jeremy pushed past her and raced down the steps. He caught Lucille by the car.

Ruby studied Jeremy as he stood in her office, looking out to the thicket of pine trees and beyond.

"I know I used to grumble about Lucille's gossip, but bringing her in gave me no pleasure," Ruby said.

"Did you believe her, when she said it was an accident?"

"Actually I do. And I also believe she's imprisoned herself every day since."

"Me too. I can't help but feel sorry for her."

"Maybe, but I feel sorrier for Eleanor. She lost her life."

"What do you think will happen?"

"I don't know. At such an advanced age with her unblemished record, probation is the most likely outcome."

"I'm sorry it ended this way, but at least we can claim total success. Arrests made in both the burglary and the murder cases. Too bad it's left only a bittersweet taste in our mouths." Jeremy turned. "Guess it's time for you to make the announcement."

"Yes." Ruby nodded her agreement. "I'll contact Bess Trundle," and she picked up the phone.

Alone now, Ruby moistened her lips. Bittersweet, Jeremy had said. It was an apt descriptor. Yes, the arrests of Stanley Kell and Lucille Trefor cleared the plate heaped high with major crimes, but her unsettled mood remained, and she knew this had little to do with the job. What was going on?

The tug of a connection with Jeremy could not

be denied. He'd claimed to want a deeper relationship with her, something she agreed she wanted, but now the official reason for him to remain in Tinker had vanished. Was there still a place for a crime analyst in the sheriff's office?

His penchant for relying on technology hadn't replaced his ability to think outside the box, something that had worried her when he first arrived. And he hadn't spent his life hiding behind machines as she first thought. Jeremy vindicated himself when he'd calmed the ruckus at the Bingo game in the Senior Center; in fact, she wasn't sure anyone else on her team would be as quick to defuse the situation.

But would the commissioners agree to extend his contract given Tinker's traditionally low crime rate? Maybe a role for a crime analyst across the county could be justified. She could guarantee he'd be an asset to any police force. Or as he'd suggested, Denver, a larger city with more job opportunities, was within commuting distance.

If he insisted on returning to New York, would she willingly relocate? No. Even though she had no immediate family in the vicinity, she'd grown attached to Tinker. She'd refused to run away after the terrible accident took her husband's life, and since her election to the office of sheriff, she'd grown even sturdier roots.

Closing the burglary and the homicide matters gave her an advantage over the few naysayers who had characterized her as an ineffective sheriff. Her tenure at the job opened doors and allowed her to meet a wide variety of people who she'd grown to love and respect. Her place was here.

But staying in Tinker alone wouldn't be easy. Ruby had grown attached to Jeremy. He'd kept the secret of her fear of heights. She could trust him on the job. She could trust him with her life.

Tell him how you feel.

It was time to trust him with her heart.

TWENTY-TWO

Jeremy put down the phone. He'd done it.

He'd come into town thinking the Tinker gig was temporary, in and out in a flash. Then he'd been told by Commissioner Tom that his career in New York was over. But when he spoke directly to his old supervisor who wanted him to hurry back, anger at the commissioner's deception replaced his initial shock. With God's help, he saw past this and dug deep to consider whether he really wanted to leave Tinker.

His attitude toward his career had changed since his arrival. He no longer considered this place a tumbleweed town. The Tinker experience opened his eyes to the wonders of having nature at his fingertips and a team of fellow crime fighters ready to join him on patrols or listen when he needed them as sounding boards for his ideas.

He'd grown accustomed to a cubicle existence in New York, at his apartment and in his work, an existence which demanded he constantly monitor his position lest someone knock him off the promotion ladder.

Immediately after he told his supervisor of his plan to remain in Tinker, a weight lifted off his shoulders. He still had to tell Ruby. Even if she didn't opt to intensify their relationship, he'd bought time to grow it slowly. He would break through her defenses until she wanted him as much as he needed her. As for future job opportunities, he would wait and listen, ever ready to follow God's plan.

"Mr. Lawson, you really are a hard act to follow. That's what New York said when they sent you our way, and they weren't kidding."

Jeremy jumped. He'd been so engrossed in thought, he hadn't heard anyone come into the office. "Commissioner Tom? What are you doing here?"

"Thought I'd drop by before the rooster crows to have a private chat. I've noticed you're often the first one in, and I'm not one to pass up opportunities, especially with my main man."

Are you watching me?

Jeremy rose from his chair. "What opportunities are you talking about?"

"The opportunity to congratulate you on arresting the burglar and then doubling down to solve the murder."

You think it reflects well because you're all about you.

"And the opportunity to follow up on my promise of rewarding you for a job well done."

"No reward necessary."

"So you say. You remember my talk of the upcoming election, don't you?"

"Ah, sure."

"You'd better look in the mirror, son, and say hello to the next sheriff."

"You're kidding."

"I've never been more serious in my life. Mind if I sit down?"

"If you must."

"If I must? That's a darn funny way of treating an admirer."

"Listen, I'm not interested in becoming the next sheriff. Tinker already has a great one who, if she runs again, is sure to be reelected."

"Don't be so sure. Ruby Prescott's in office for the sole reason that her predecessor was a fella who'd grown stale to the public eye after two terms. In my opinion she lacks some essential skills."

Jeremy remembered Lucille's compliment of Ruby the first time they'd interviewed her. "I've heard some people say she cleaned things up."

"Hah. Not much to clean up in my opinion. In fact, the time and attention it took to investigate allegations of possible wrongdoing that amounted to nothing ate up much needed time and effort to keep a lid on crime."

"Are you saying the crime rate rose after Ruby became sheriff?"

"Seemed that way to me, but you could look at the statistics, satisfy yourself."

Jeremy wondered how much stock to put in the commissioner's words. After all, this same man had told him he was now persona non grata in New York, and he knew better. Still, it always paid to be diplomatic.

"I'll take your word for it, but if there was a significant increase in the crime rate, I'm sure it was attributable to several other factors, not just to who held the position of sheriff."

"Look at her record. When you arrived, she'd already spent six months trying to catch a serial burglar with nothing to show for it. Speaks for itself."

"I can say, based on my observations, Ruby is one hardworking sheriff. Best I've seen. I'm sure she would have figured out the burglar's pattern of targeting places on her own."

"But she didn't, and that's my point. She kept coming up empty. You solved it in six weeks."

"Part of it was luck."

"Don't sell yourself short. You solved the case of the skeleton in the trunk too."

"No, Ruby and I solved it together. It's called teamwork."

"Your loyalty to Ruby and her team speaks in your favor, but on top of cracking our major cases, you've managed to gather a core group of people who'd vote for you as sheriff in a heartbeat."

"You're referring to Lucille's cohorts." He tried to tamp down his incredulity.

"Don't discount them. They carry sway in the community, and that amounts to a lot of votes."

"I don't want votes. I'm salaried."

"That could change." Commissioner Tom could barely conceal the menace in his voice.

"Are you threatening me?"

"Me threaten you? Don't be absurd. All I'm saying is every commissioner votes to appoint deputies, and I don't always have a lot of sway over my colleagues. Personally, I'm hoping you stay on our force, but I know, in addition to being a team player, you've got the capabilities to head up the whole thing."

"Let me speak plainly. I do not want the job of sheriff."

"Not even if it's the only way we keep Ruby on the payroll?"

"What are you implying?"

"I'll say it straight up. A few people, including me, have doubts about our esteemed sheriff. But if you were elected to the office and pushed Ruby forward as a deputy, a lot of those same people could climb on that wagon to buy what you're trying to sell."

Jeremy wondered how long he'd have to stand

there and feign interest in what Commissioner Tom was saying.

The commissioner's voice droned on. "I gave you two tasks. One was to make an arrest in the serial burglary case. You did that in record time. The other was to get enough dirt on Queen Ruby to propel her from her comfy chair. Keep her out of my hair, such as it is." He patted the bald spot on the top of his head.

Jeremy gritted his teeth. Muckraking seemed to go hand in hand with Commissioner Tom, but even though his anger at this attitude threatened to boil over, he had to consider maybe the commissioner really didn't understand Ruby's situation.

"Pardon me, sir, but I think she's overcome a lot and, for that reason alone, deserves everyone's respect, especially yours."

"What do you mean?" The commissioner leaned forward and rested his elbows on his thighs, adopting a serious conversation pose.

"She's lived with a truckload of grief since her husband's death and has the scars to show it. She's coped with anxiety, even had a full-blown panic attack. But through it all, she's continued to do an excellent job."

"Panic attack? I had no idea."

"It's only happened once. Looking down from a height at the squash court triggered a small problem."

"A fear of heights could really get in the way

of doing a good job." Commissioner Tom's eyes glittered. "Well, well, well." He rubbed his hands together.

"Wait a minute." Jeremy narrowed his eyes. "The panic attack didn't get in the way, that's what I'm telling you. I mentioned the incident hoping you'd cut Ruby some slack. She certainly deserves it."

"Now, son, I think you know better. I'm not in the habit of cutting some slack, as you say. I'm in the habit of expecting and receiving the best. And the best is what you've delivered. Panic attacks don't bode well for anyone tasked with upholding the law, so congratulations. You just delivered the dirt I need to get rid of Ruby."

Jeremy shook his head. "You're taking what I said out of context."

"I think not. Maybe what we're looking at here is low self-esteem on your part, caused by the mistake in New York. Maybe you think there'd be no point in running for sheriff next election because you wouldn't win. But I've got news. You'll win by a landslide. I'll see to it."

I don't want to run. I don't want to win. I won't run.

"I have no interest in winning, either by a smidge or a landslide."

"You have to run. I'll nominate you and you'll have no choice. How else could you afford to stay in Tinker? The sheriff's position is the only avenue for promotion with a salary that could come close to what you used to pull in at your old job. And think of all the citizens of Tinker you'd disappoint if you remain in the background and let Ruby Prescott continue to steal the limelight."

"I don't have to stand here and listen to this."

"No? You're in it up to your elbows, Jeremy. I positioned you here, and I will decide whether or not you run for sheriff in the next election. You solved the biggest case that's dogged us for a half year and given me enough information to undermine Ruby Prescott. You really are my main man."

As Commissioner Tom guffawed, Jeremy heard a door slam. He looked up in time to see Ruby running away from the office. His heart sank. She must've heard some if not all of what the commissioner had said.

No, no, no. He had to go after her, to explain. Jeremy pushed past Commissioner Tom and raced out the door.

So Jeremy was Tom Ewan's main man. She'd heard it herself. Jeremy, the man to whom she planned to give her heart, was a plant. Tears streamed down her face. Ruby ran with no direction, stumbling at first but then catching her balance and gathering speed. Down the incline, over the frozen grass, dirt and rocks, on and on until she fell to the ground, out of breath. Sobs wracked her body.

Finally she stopped heaving and pulled herself up to a sitting position. Her heart sank. Guilty of poor judgment, again. What she'd thought was real was fictitious. But then logic prevailed. How could she have believed another person would overlook her shortcomings when she couldn't overlook them herself?

When she'd chosen to drive home through one of the worst storms in Tinker's history instead of waiting it out at a motel, like her husband suggested, she endangered them both. On top of that, she'd failed to keep her husband safe.

After he passed, Ruby drifted, but a lifestyle funded by insurance payouts drained her of purpose. She needed redemption, to prove she was capable of caring for the community and keeping it safe.

Focusing on her strengths instead of defining herself by her weaknesses, Ruby took a bold step and declared herself a candidate in the last election. Through hard work and with God's help she learned to forgive herself just as He had surely forgiven her.

True, when she'd taken office, rumors swirled about two sets of enforcement protocols for one set of laws. Ruby, who couldn't tolerate double standards or favoritism, took immediate action. And made enemies. But she'd never suspected the upshot would be for an adversary like Commissioner Tom to plant someone in the sheriff's office.

When she met Jeremy, his infatuation with computers, unfamiliarity with nature and methods of investigation that relied on statistics instead of common sense gave her plenty of reason to push him away. But he'd inched his way into her head with his sometimes comical mistakes and missteps, and eventually she'd lowered her defenses and allowed him to get close to her heart.

Her chest ached. She'd given Jeremy access only to find he fed information to her enemies and coveted her job. Had he been thrilled by his newfound control, knowing he could ingratiate himself and con her into divulging her secrets? She dropped her head and sobbed.

TWENTY-THREE

"I knew I'd find you in the churchyard." Jeremy spoke quietly, but still Ruby shuddered.

She looked around and recognized the familiar redbrick building flanked with now fallow flower beds. How frequently she'd walked up the buff flagstone path and through the wooden doors to hear the word of the Lord and receive His sustenance.

Jeremy claimed a spot next to Ruby and reached for her hand. "Please?"

Ruby trembled from the wave of emotions that flooded through her system. She yearned to unhear what she'd heard but couldn't.

He squeezed her hand. She forced herself to look at him.

"It's not what you think," he began.

"What do I think?"

"That I was sent to the office to spy on you. It may have been on Commissioner Tom's agenda, but it was never my intention."

"Why were you sent to Tinker?"

"I was supposed to redeem myself and assist you by adding a unique voice to this milieu. If my skills made a difference, I could reclaim my position as a top crime analyst and return to New York a hero."

"I remember you told me that earlier. At least your story's consistent."

"It's consistent because it's true. When we apprehended the burglar and solved the murder, I was invited to go back. But I talked to them this morning—before Commissioner Tom ambushed me in the office. I said no to New York. I'm staying here."

Her hand trembled in his. She wanted to believe him.

"I overheard him say you're an automatic win in the election if you stay and run against me."

"Commissioner Tom's constructed a fantasy. He started from the position I'm here at his behest. But I am not in his debt."

"No?"

"No. Sometimes our interests have been the same. We both wanted to see the serial burglar stopped, but our motivations differed. He believed burglaries that terrorized the town reflected poorly on him as a commissioner, but he couldn't have cared less about the homicide. In his opinion, the murder was too old to cast a shadow on his tenure, ergo no threat. He resented any time being spent on tracking down the killer so long as the burglary case remained outstanding."

"Commissioner Tom's a narcissist."

"You don't say?" Jeremy pretended surprise.

"Anyway, my mandate is to solve crimes. Of course, now that an arrest has been made in both cases, it's easy for him to claim credit for bringing me here. And that fits with his plan to have me run for the sheriff's office in the next election, which is why he asked me to gather dirt on you. I'm sad to say I inadvertently told him about your fear of heights."

Ruby swallowed.

"He tricked me, manipulated me into thinking he'd be less derogatory toward you if he understood some of the obstacles you've faced."

"So, that's why he gloated about gaining an advantage over me."

Jeremy paused and licked his lips before continuing. "I know you went to great lengths to conceal what you consider a blemish. I also know you sought professional help to overcome your fear. But isn't the goal of therapy to be okay with who you are now? Ruby, you cannot undo the past, but you can embrace the person you are today. You solved what could be the worst crime spree in Tinker's history, laid a skeleton to rest, and still had time to help me adjust to a new life. Pretty stupendous from where I'm standing. So does it matter that you still dislike heights and probably always will?"

Ruby hit pause and sat in silence while she considered Jeremy's words.

"You're saying you think it's time to accept myself?"

"Affirmative. And I know the ability to be okay with who you are is your greatest attraction and your best defense. If you act from a base of authenticity, all the mud Commissioner Tom slings will slide off and form that puddle on the sidewalk that people avoid when they have to walk in the rain. Of course that same advice holds for me."

"It does?"

"Yep. The prospect that I'd made a mistake in my profiling work terrified me. It impacted my career. I became anxious and irritable. I was no good to me or anyone else. But being in Tinker has taught me to take pleasure in the small victories and not to demand perfection from myself. God doesn't expect perfection. He just asks that we try to be our best selves."

"Jeremy Lawson, I had no idea you were so people savvy."

"I'm not always, but I've had a lot of time to think, and I have a plan."

"Oh?"

"A lot of people want a career as a crime analyst in the Big Apple. I was ambitious, determined to prove my superiority until I transferred to Tinker."

"The path less traveled?"

"Something like that. I still figured solving both cases was the ticket back to my old life. But the longer I stayed, the more I saw Tinker as my fork in the road, my way for a new life, a better one."

"How? Unless you run against me for the sheriff's office, you may have already reached the height of your career."

"Yeah, yeah. That's what the commissioner thinks too. But it's not true."

"No?"

"In the words of someone dear to me, nope." Jeremy smiled. "When I first laid eyes on you, I saw you were special. I knew we got off on the wrong foot, but as the weeks turned into a month, I hoped you'd see me not as the bumbling city boy hiding behind software but as a man worthy of your trust and romantic attention."

"So, what are you going to do when Commissioner Tom nominates you to run in the election?"

"Decline. I've got no interest in the job, not when a great sheriff is already in place. My interest lies in helping you get reelected, and if I have as much sway with the good folks of Tinker as the commissioner thinks, it should be easy to convince them you are the best candidate."

Jeremy's words lifted her spirits. Ruby wanted to believe him with all her heart. When she recalled how he jumped into the Casper rapids and torpedoed over the falls after her unsuccessful wrestling match with the burglar, her heart melted.

His behavior, like the time he drove out to buy her a hot coffee on the coldest day of the month, embodied his devotion to her. His grin, ever present at each aha moment after she'd puzzled out the solution to a thorny problem embodied his affinity to the crime-solving process.

"Are you sure you want to alienate Commissioner Tom? He makes a potent enemy. I know from experience."

Jeremy bowed his head and took a deep breath before speaking. "What kind of man do you think I am that I would cower and run at the onset of trouble? I'll take on Commissioner Tom or anybody who dares to undermine you, Ruby."

"Strong words, but what if the crime rate in Tinker slows and there's not enough work for a crime analyst?"

Jeremy took both hands in hers. "I'm sure I'll find work, whether in Tinker, the county, even Denver. I may not know all the details of God's plan for me, but I do know He has one. It's up to me to be open and to listen."

Ruby nodded and allowed Jeremy to pull her to standing.

"It's you I want, Ruby Prescott. I knew it when I met you, and everything that's transpired only served to convince me I'm on target." He stopped and gazed at her. "Please accept me, Ruby. I love you with my whole heart, today and always. With God's support and you by my side, we can overcome any obstacle. Please, let's be a couple, me and you."

The sun broke through a cloud and a shaft of light encircled them. Ruby was blessed. She thought of all the ups and downs of the last few months, how Jeremy had stood by her through it all. She trusted and respected him. His smile, his jokes, his intelligence made her heart sing.

"Yes," she said. "I love you too."

And then she kissed him.

EPILOGUE

Three Months Later

It was a day so bright even dogs were outfitted with wraparound sun goggles. There was a record turnout at the polling stations, but the final tally surprised no one. The commissioners, the mayor, and Sheriff Ruby Prescott were all reelected.

Stanley Kell's contributions to the community were taken into consideration at his sentencing for the burglaries. He was ordered to attend addiction counseling, and part of his mandated community service included training white-water rafters and teaching boat safety.

As one of the terms of her sentence, Lucille Trefor agreed to tear down the old Grand Theater and replace it with a butterfly sanctuary. "Eleanor loved all that fluttered," she said.

Harvey Klingshot kept busy with a full production schedule at the theater and continued to beseech Ruby and Jeremy to join him onstage in an amateur production.

Because there was not enough crime to sustain an analyst in Tinker alone, Jeremy's redesignated job encompassed responsibility for the whole county.

Ruby and Jeremy set a wedding date for the fourth Saturday in May. They settled on th grounds in Rock Garden Park as a venue. The Kissing Camels would form the perfect background for their nuptials, and Pastor Emeritus Henry Miller would preside.

Once Jeremy had vowed to love her and be there for her forever, Ruby knew she had found her perfect world at last.

* * * * *

Dear Reader,

I hope you enjoyed reading the story of Ruby and Jeremy as much as I enjoyed writing it.

No writer works alone and there are many I have to thank. This includes my agent, the late Dawn Dowdle, and Lynette Eason, who critiqued my first chapter. Hugs go out to my sister and my dog for providing unending support for my work.

Heartfelt thanks to the Harlequin team who answered all my questions and offered sage suggestions throughout the process. And a wink to Denise Cook, who has the best fist pumps ever.

Change, whether from technological advances or unanticipated disruptions to our plans, can seem overwhelming. But if we accept God's helping hand and learn to reach out, together, we can forge new paths and find love and peace, and hopefully romance, along the way.

God bless.
Carol